LOST AND GOWNED

ROSEMARY'S WEDDING

MELISSA F. MILLER

Published by Brown Street Books.

Brown Street Books ISBN: 978-1-940759-28-9

For Rosie.

CHAPTER 1

*I*t was nearly two o'clock in the morning when I finally returned home from catering the Steinbrenner-Moskowitzes' four-hundred-person wedding reception in Laurel Canyon. I dragged myself to the bathroom to brush my teeth. You could say I was bone tired; but that would be an understatement. I was bone, skin, muscle, organ, and blood cell tired. Even my *hair* was tired.

It was all I could do to lift the toothbrush to my mouth to give my teeth a half-hearted two minutes of brushing. The muscles in my right arm burned from the effort. Flossing was out of the question. My only thought was of my bed. I couldn't wait to flop my head on my soft, fluffy pillow and burrow under my comforter to settle in for a dreamless sleep.

I turned to trudge from the bathroom to the bedroom and bumped into the wall of muscle that was my boyfriend Dave's chest.

"Hey," I managed in a monotone.

"Hey, yourself." He planted a kiss on the top of my head. "It looked like the reception went off without a hitch," he observed as he trailed me into the bedroom.

I smiled weakly. He was right. The wedding reception had been, well, perfect.

Every detail—from the pearls woven into the bride's bouquet to the sugar globes and gold leaf studding the four-tier wedding cake—had been fine-tuned and fussed over, thanks in no small part to the mother of the bride's obsessive attention to every imaginable detail. The florist and the band-leader had found Mrs. Steinbrenner to be irritating at worst and distracting at best, but I thought her behavior was sort of endearing. She just wanted to make sure her daughter's big day was perfect, after all. It was hardly a war crime.

Dave had caught the very end of the reception, as the guests had waved goodbye to the happy couple under a canopy of fairy lights and gardenias. Then, he'd helped me schlep all my stuff to my car and his pickup truck and had caravanned down the canyon hills with me.

"It was a beautiful wedding. It nearly killed me, but it was glorious. I never want to *think* about another wedding again. Ever."

Dave gave a short nod of his head. "Right."

I loved owning my own catering company. Feeding people filled my soul. But I felt this way—flattened and drained—after every wedding, so Dave could be forgiven for ignoring my hyperbole.

"I mean it this time. No more weddings," I insisted, stifling a yawn.

Instead of challenging my empty statement, he just took me by the hand, led me to the edge of the bed, and gently pushed me into a seated position.

"Rosemary, before you go to sleep tonight, there's one more thing I want to do."

I stared up at him for a long, bleary moment. I mean, don't get me wrong—I'm very into my boyfriend, but he *had* to be kidding. I was exhausted.

"Not tonight, pal. I'm dead on my feet." I tried to soften the blow with a smile and gentle pat on his forearm. "I'd love a rain check for tomorrow, though," I said in my best sexy voice, which given the hour and my state was pretty ragged.

He fixed me with an expression of mild disdain and shook his head. "Not *that*."

I looked at him blankly with heavy-lidded, sleepy eyes. If not *that,* then what? What did he want to do in the middle of the night after I'd worked an eighteen-hour day on the heels of back-to-back fifteen-hour workdays? Play Scrabble? Give the dog a bath? As I was formulating my witty retort, he dropped to one knee on the bedroom floor.

I cocked my head and stared at him in confusion. From her spot on the foot of the bed, our dog, Mona Lisa, gave him an equally quizzical head tilt. I yawned, wide-mouthed, and tried to make sense of the whole scene but my fuzzy brain wouldn't cooperate.

He reached into his pocket and produced a tiny, square box tied with a white satin bow.

My eyes popped all the way open. My pulse fluttered. I took a quick sniff of my fingers to see if I caught a whiff of the two dozen heads of garlic I'd roasted for my silky garlic and herb dip. Luckily, my trick of rubbing my hands with a lemon after handling garlic seemed to have worked. I didn't smell like vampire repellant, as far as I could tell.

Dave intertwined his fingers between mine. Then he smiled, and his warm brown eyes crinkled adorably.

"I love you, Rosemary. I love every ludicrous thing about you. I love your gross fast food habit, your stubbornness, the way you drool in your sleep."

"I don't drool," I protested, even though we both knew my pillow was damp every morning.

He ignored me and plowed ahead with his speech. "I want to spend every day for the rest of my life watching you drool. Will you marry me, Rosemary?"

He returned my hand to my lap and opened the box. A slender band with a sparkling stone that caught the light like water sat nestled on a white silk pillow.

I was definitely wide awake now. In fact, I was bouncing on the edge of the bed like a kid. Pure joy shot through me. I forgot all about my tired, achy, exhausted self and was struck by three immediate, phenomenal ideas.

One, *of course* I would marry him. I loved Dave Drummond beyond all reason. We'd woven our lives together so seamlessly that I couldn't imagine my world without him in it.

Two, I couldn't wait to bake my own wedding cake. I already knew exactly what flavors I'd use— honeysuckle lemon cake with lavender cream, topped with crystallized wildflowers.

And three, we would have the wedding at Tranquility, the Resort by the Sea, the struggling vacation retreat I co-owned with my sisters Sage and Thyme.

In hindsight, one of three would actually turn out to be a good idea. The other two? Disastrous, calamitous, catastrophic. Plain old bad.

Oblivious to the storm to come, I flung my arms around his neck and squeaked out an excited 'yes.'

CHAPTER 2

SAGE

I was brushing my teeth when my phone vibrated across the vanity. I grabbed it with my free hand and noted the name on the display: *Rosemary*.

My stomach clenched. It was just about six a.m. here, which meant it was the middle of the night in Los Angeles. *Why would Rosemary be calling me at three o'clock in the morning?*

I hurriedly spat my toothpaste into the basin and rinsed out my mouth.

"Rosemary? What's wrong?"

She giggled. "Nothing. Absolutely nothing in the world is wrong. In fact, everything's perfect!"

"Are you drunk?"

"What? No."

As far as I knew, my older sister didn't use drugs, but I asked anyway. "High?"

"I'm high on life, Sage." More giggling.

"Oh-kay. Um ..."

"I have news! But I'm so tired from catering a wedding all night that I can't figure out how to conference in Thyme. Will you do it?"

I glanced at the clock on my phone. "I'll try. But she's probably already working with her first client."

Apparently, in New York, the more affluent and powerful you were, the more likely you were to be doing planks and lunges before the sun was fully up. I liked the Hilton Head Island approach better. Here, the rich and famous slept in, golfed, and then bummed around the beach until cocktail hour.

I put Rosemary on hold and hit the speed dial button for Thyme's number. She answered on the second ring. Based on the cacophony of car horns, beeping trucks, and the roar of engines, she was out walking around.

"Hey, what's up?"

"Can you talk?"

"Not really. There was a mechanical problem on the subway, so the trains are delayed. And it's raining, of course, so there are no cabs to be had. I'm hoofing it to the Upper West Side for an appointment. I'm going to have to run, literally."

"You couldn't pay me to live there."

"Greatest city in the world, sis. Can I call you this afternoon?"

"I have Rosemary on hold. She asked me to conference you in."

"Rosie? It's three o'clock in the morning there. Is she okay?"

"I don't know. She sounds weird."

Thyme sighed. "Okay, add her to the call. Everybody else in this city blames the weather when they're late. I suppose I can, too."

"Hang on." I pressed the conference button to loop in our loopy older sister. "Rosemary?" I asked to confirm I hadn't disconnected her.

"Yep!" she chirped.

"Thyme?"

"I'm here." Thyme's voice was cautious. "So, you obviously have news or you wouldn't be calling so early. The only question is whether it's bad news or horrible news."

9

I felt myself nodding. If she was calling to tell us about yet another expensive disaster at the resort I would just sit down and cry right here on the bathroom floor. We'd been pouring as much money into Tranquility by the Sea as we could. But something or another was constantly breaking or malfunctioning. Or flooding. Or being eaten by termites.

"It's the best news," she assured us. "Dave and I are getting married!"

Thyme and I both started squealing and laughing at the same time.

After a minute, I calmed down and said, "I'm so happy for you! You two are great together." I wondered if my giant smile might split my face in half.

"Dave's the best," Thyme added. "This is so exciting!"

"I know! I'm never going to get to sleep at this rate. So, listen, will you be my co-maids of honor?"

"Of course!" I said.

"Do you even have to ask? Yes!" Thyme chimed in.

"We're going to have so much fun getting the resort ready for a wedding!" Rosemary enthused.

There was a long silence.

"Sage? Thyme? Did I lose you?"

"Um, no, I'm here. Did you say you want to have the wedding at the resort? *Our* down-at-the-heels resort?" I asked.

"It's charming," she shot back.

Thyme cleared her throat. "It has a certain shabby chic vibe," she said diplomatically. "But, let's be honest, it's more shabby than chic."

"Besides, do you really want to plan a wedding in New Jersey all the way from California? Wouldn't it be easier logistically to have it out there? Maybe Napa Valley?" I suggested.

Rosemary's temper flared. "I want to be married in our childhood home. I want to use the money I would otherwise spend to rent a venue to spruce up the resort a bit. And I want you to support my idea, for Pete's sake!"

"No need to go full Bridezilla this early in the process," Thyme muttered.

I choked back a laugh and tried to soothe the savage bride. "Of course, it's *your* day. I mean, yours and Dave's. Is he on board with getting hitched at the resort?"

"Yes."

"Well, then it's settled."

"Listen, Rosemary, I am so super thrilled for you. And Sage is right. You can get married in a laundromat for all I care. I just want to be a part of your amazing day, okay?"

"Okay."

"Okay. I *have* to go. Cate is going to be apoplectic if she doesn't have time for a full yoga asana series today. I love you both." Thyme made kissing noises into the phone.

"Bye. I love you both, too."

"Love you both. Hey, before you go—-make sure you text us a picture of the ring," I said.

"I will," she promised.

Thyme and I waited until the phone sounded three short *bip bip bip* noises. Then she said, "Rosie?"

No response.

"She hung up," I confirmed with a glance at my phone's display. "So ..."

"Yeah."

"I mean, it *is* her wedding. And she'll probably be able to keep costs down if we do it at the resort. But, still ..."

"Yep."

There was a silence while we both considered the myriad disasters that could befall a wedding at the resort. As it turns out, the one that actually happened was wilder than anything I managed to imagine.

CHAPTER 3

THYME

*A*fter Rosemary's middle-of-the-night call, things happened fast. She flew out to New York the next weekend to hammer out a game plan for the wedding. New York was the most logical place to meet. It was a direct flight from LAX, and it was a short drive from my apartment to the resort, provided we didn't hit any traffic. Which, of course, we did.

Sage had really wanted to come up from South Carolina to join us, but the Moores, the family she worked for, had some big public appearance for a charity Chip had established to help Gullah Geechee children. So she couldn't get away. That hadn't stopped her from texting me dozens of ideas, suggestions, and reminders to share with Rosemary.

The day after Rosemary landed, we spent a long, boring afternoon picking out invitations. I never in my life would have thought there were so many different kinds of paper. Vellum, parchment, card stock, fabric, the list went on. My mind was reeling when we left the stationery store.

"How about a drink?" I proposed, half-dazed.

"Good grief, yes."

So, over a couple well-earned glasses of Scotch at the bar around the corner from my apartment, I pulled up Sage's greatest hits and started running them by Rosemary.

She made decisions like an empress. Instantaneously, decisively, swiftly.

"S'mores bar?"

"Yes."

"Chalkboard menu?"

"No."

"Fairy lights in the trees?"

"Yes."

"A dress from Chelle's?"

"Yes."

"Parsley as feline ring bearer?"

"Uh, no." She snorted.

"Harpist for the ceremony musician?"

"Sure."

I paused. "Do you want to run any of this by Dave?"

"Nah." She sipped her Scotch. "He wants veto power over the menu, but other than that, the reception's all mine. He's in charge of the ceremony. He lined up a friend to officiate, and he's busy picking out readings."

"Okay, great." I scanned the texts and my stomach dropped. "Um, what about the guest list?"

She tilted her head. "What about it? Sage already has it set up in some fancy database, doesn't she?"

I fussed with my glass.

"Are you stalling, Thyme?"

I wished Victor were here. Rosemary would never cause a scene in front of my boyfriend. But he was on a deadline for a long-form article. I was on my own. If I didn't ask her, Sage would. And I knew from experience that conversation would go *way* worse.

I squared my shoulders and said, "Have you considered inviting Mom and Dad?"

Then I waited for her to erupt. But she didn't.

Instead she grew very, very quiet, lifted her

chin, and said in a voice devoid of expression, "I don't have an address for Mom and Dad. And I don't want one. The people who matter to me will be invited to the wedding. The people who don't, won't. You can tell Sage the guest list is final."

I gulped down my drink and nodded, afraid to say another word on the subject. I savored the smooth, fiery Scotch while silently cursing Sage for putting me in Rosemary's crosshairs.

CHAPTER 4

ROSEMARY

*D*ave and I pulled into the resort's circular driveway in near-total darkness. Our flight from LAX had been delayed. Then there'd been storms over Illinois with lots of stomach-jostling turbulence. By the time we rented a car at Newark Airport and pointed it toward the Seashore area, I was drained and cranky.

As soon as the car bumped off the highway and onto resort property, I felt my tension melting away. That was the thing about Tranquility, the Resort by the Sea. Despite its warts, it held a definite, palpable magic. I buzzed down my window to drink in the salty night air. Then I turned to Dave to see if he felt it, too.

"Look at that," he exclaimed, pointing to the

front garden. Hundreds and hundreds of fireflies flitted through the high grass and native plants, their bioluminescent tails glowing like tiny, flickering lanterns in the night.

I grinned. Oh, yeah, he felt it, too.

"I hope the fireflies will come out for the wedding. They're so wild and delicately beautiful at the same time."

"Just like you," he said in a deep voice that caught in his throat.

My pulse quickened. Before I could respond, the sconces on both sides of the wide oak front door came to life, and Sage, Thyme, and their boyfriends poured out onto the wraparound porch, trailed by the family cat. Sage was clutching a bottle of wine, and Thyme held a tray of glasses.

"I think we're about to be toasted and fêted," I said.

He parked the car and smiled at me. "I can't think of a better way to kick off our wedding weekend, can you?"

I kissed him softly. "I can't think of a better way to kick off our life together."

We got out of the car to shouts of greeting and good wishes. My eyes filled with joyful tears. Everything was perfect. Or nearly so.

CHAPTER 5

SAGE

I was perched on a stool watching Rosemary assemble a massive salad. I'd offered to help her, but she'd shooed me away with the corner of her apron as if she were a farmer's wife and I were a chicken. According to her, it would be quicker if she did it herself. "I'm still not sure what made you decide to cater your own wedding," I mused as I eyed the tray of cheese, nuts, and olives on the counter.

As if on cue, my stomach growled. I just needed her to turn around to get something out of the refrigerator so I could snag a handful of munchies without getting caught. But she must've been using her oldest sister insight to guess what I had in mind because she hadn't turned her back to me at any point in the past ten minutes.

"Don't be so dramatic—I'm only catering the rehearsal lunch. And the reason it's a good idea is because it saves us a ton of money."

I frowned. It seemed unfair that Rosemary's big day had such strong budgetary constraints surrounding it. But the truth was, the resort hadn't been doing great. We'd spent so much money paying off the debt we'd inherited that we had very little leftover for upkeep and improvements to the property, and it was starting to show. So, as one-third co-owner, I was glad she was funneling her spare cash into the resort and not her wedding. But still.

She caught my eye and smiled as though she could tell what I was thinking—again.

"It's fine," she insisted as she whisked oil, herbs, and red wine vinegar in a big glass bowl, her arm moving so quickly that her hand was a blur. "To be honest, I find it very relaxing. Focusing on the menu is warding off any pre-wedding jitters."

That actually made a good bit of sense. Rosemary did seem to approach cooking with a meditative bent. But, while she may have been having tomorrow's meal catered, she had insisted she was making her own wedding cake. She'd gone and dug out some recipe of our mom's that I didn't even remember—and I'm the family historian.

"Are you nervous?"

"Only about whether the cake's going to turn out." She laughed.

"Are you *sure* you don't want to farm out the cake? Pretty Pastries over in Ocean Dunes would squeeze in a rush order for you. They'd be happy to do it."

Rosemary waved away my concern with her hand.

"Have you even ever made this honeysuckle lavender concoction before?" I asked, taking one last shot.

"I was just kidding about being worried about it. It'll be a piece of cake. Ha ha. Get it?"

I shook my head. Rosemary was the stubborn one. There was no sense arguing with her. My stomach rumbled again. I decided to risk her wrath and popped an olive into my mouth. She narrowed her eyes but didn't say anything.

I decided a change of subject was in order. "So how's Dave? Getting excited?"

Her fiancé wasn't really the excitable type. But Rosemary brought out the boyish side of the straight-laced homicide detective. He'd been roaming around the resort, laughing and slapping people on their backs good-naturedly.

"I think so. I hope so. He's got to pick up the officiant before the rehearsal lunch but right now he's probably having a blast with Roman and Victor."

I gave her a blank look. My boyfriend had been gone when I'd woken up, and I hadn't the faintest idea where he'd gone. "Why? What are they doing?"

"They left early to do some deep sea fishing. Roman didn't want to wake you because you never get to sleep late."

I smiled. Roman was the best. I loved being a nanny, but the early morning hours were a definite drawback to my job. So when I got the chance to sleep in, I made it a point to take advantage of it.

"I'm glad the three of them get along." I couldn't imagine if my boyfriend didn't like my sisters' significant others. Can you say 'deal breaker?'

Rosemary nodded, focused on composing her salad. "Me, too." She kept talking, not looking up, half to herself, half to me. "So I need to do my final fitting after lunch," she told me.

As co-maid of honor I had been in charge of coordinating with the seamstress. I wrinkled my forehead at her. I definitely hadn't scheduled a fitting for the bride the day of the rehearsal. I pulled out my phone to check my calendar. "I thought you already had a final fitting."

She nodded a yes and tasted her dressing before answering me. "I did. But I think the stress has caught up with me. I may have dropped a pound or two."

"Stress?" She'd just said she wasn't nervous.

"Excitement," she corrected herself.

Rosemary was known to forget to eat during times of high stress. It was not a problem I personally had, as I seemed to be able to remember to eat no matter what was happening in my life. But if Rosie had been under pressure, she'd probably dropped more than a pound or two.

I regarded her carefully. Her elbows *were* looking particularly sharp and bony, but I decided not to point it out—I was afraid she might jab me in the side with one of them.

"Thyme and I will go with you. What time is Chelle expecting you to come in?"

"She said she'd come here so I don't have to drag the dress into town."

"That's nice of her," I said.

"It is. So I invited her to join us for lunch. We can do the fitting right after we finish up with the meal."

That was also like Rosemary. She loved to feed people. Before I could ask her just how many extra guests she'd invited to this rehearsal lunch, my co-maid of honor, our youngest sister Thyme, burst through the doorway into the kitchen, out of breath and wild-eyed.

CHAPTER 6

THYME

I hustled into the big kitchen out of breath and flustered because I was running so late. I must've slammed the door harder than I'd intended because Rosemary wheeled around to stare at me as I entered.

I noted that Sage took advantage of the distraction to steal a handful of cheese and nuts from the nearest tray—a risky move, if you asked me. Rosemary had been very clear: she'd bought just enough food for the rehearsal luncheon. I gave Sage a warning look. She shrugged her shoulders and made a sheepish face.

"Is everything okay?" she asked me around a mouthful of cheddar.

I cut my eyes toward Rosemary before I answered.

As the youngest sister I'd had the fewest responsibilities with regard to wedding planning. Sage had taken on a lot of the work and Rosemary, being Rosemary, had done a lot of it herself. But one of my jobs—probably my most important job— was to handle the venue issues. You'd think it would be an easy job since we owned the venue.

Yet, here I was, thirty-six hours before the wedding ceremony was set to take place, bearing bad news. I filled my lungs with air and then blurted, "I guess there's been some sort of miscommunication with Kay."

"What kind of miscommunication?" Rosemary wanted to know. She didn't look up at me but kept slicing through the cucumbers from the resort's sprawling vegetable garden in a fast, even rhythm.

"I'm really not sure how it happened. I thought I was crystal clear with Kay that she shouldn't book any reservations this weekend. Even though we don't need all the rooms for the guests, I thought it would be nicer if you had the resort to yourself. You know, for privacy."

Rosemary nodded her agreement, which was no surprise. She was a very private person. And,

Kay, the sweetest lady you'd ever want to meet, had known us forever, loved us like daughters, and understood Rosie's reserved personality. Plus, Kay was usually a super-competent reservations manager. But, here we were.

"Kay booked a couple in the garden cottage. A Mr. and Mrs. Simon. I just happened to be coming back from checking on the tent set up when I saw them at the registration desk. They're ornithology buffs. They're here to do some bird watching, according to Kay. I tried to catch them to tell them there's a family function going on this weekend. But they hustled off to their room really quickly before I had a chance to speak to them."

I'd really tried, too, but they had virtually sprinted out of the building when I called their names. I looked from one of my sisters to the other, trying to gauge their reactions.

"I could stop by the cottage and offer to book them in the bed and breakfast in town on our dime?" I suggested. I didn't know what else to do.

Rosemary seemed to be considering the idea, but Sage was the one who answered.

"No, don't do that. It's not worth risking the bad review on the travel websites. It was an honest mistake, and it's just one older couple. How much of a disruption or distraction could they really be? Especially if they're off bird watching in the marshes. Just let it go, Thyme."

Rosemary puffed out a breath before adding her agreement. "She's right."

I exhaled, relieved that they weren't angry at the oversight. Then I tilted my head and looked at our middle sister. "How did you know they were an older couple?"

Sage gave me a long, blank look. Rosemary paused. The Parmesan cheese she was shaving over the salad hovered in the air as she waited to hear Sage's answer.

After a moment, Sage blinked. "I don't know. I guess I just assumed birding isn't really a young person's hobby," she said in a hesitant voice.

"Well, you guessed right," I told her.

Judging from the glimpse I'd had of their backs as they scurried through the lobby, the Simons seemed to be in their late sixties or so. It was hard to tell, though, with those big-brimmed hats they'd both been wearing.

"Besides, it's not like we can't use the money from the booking," Rosemary continued, bringing the conversation back to the booking. "In fact, as long as we reserve the main house for the wedding guests, we might as well go ahead and tell Kay to open up the rest of the cottages for last-minute reservations, too."

"Are you sure?" I asked.

Rosemary nodded.

I shrugged. "Okay, I'll let Kay know."

That conversation had gone more smoothly than I'd expected it to. I'd anticipated getting a lecture from Sage, at a minimum. But, I wasn't going to argue with them. In fact, I was going to hightail it out of there before Rosemary changed her mind.

As I headed for the door, Sage called after me, "Hey, Thyme, Rosemary needs to have one final fitting. Chelle is going to come out and join us for the rehearsal lunch then put the finishing touches on Rosemary's dress. So keep your late afternoon open if you want to be there."

I had planned to take a walk along the beach with Victor and point out all my childhood haunts. But he seemed to be hitting it off with Dave and with Sage's boyfriend Roman. The three of them could grab a beer or something while Chelle fussed over Rosemary's dress.

I didn't want to miss the fitting. It would be one last sisters-only event before Rosemary got married. Rosemary, married. I could hardly believe it was really happening. For the briefest second, I wished our parents could be there to see it, too. But I brushed the thought away before it even had a chance to fully form.

"Of course, I'll be there. And, Sage, you might want to save some of those snacks for the appetizer table," I added over my shoulder as I left.

I turned back in time to see Sage shooting me a dirty look. I had to laugh—between her cheeks stuffed full of nuts and her glare, she looked like a furious, demented squirrel.

CHAPTER 7

ROSEMARY

I stood under the old sycamore tree at the crest of the sloping hill in the backyard and gazed out at the sea grass and the Atlantic beyond. Twinkling lights had been wound through the tree limbs and would cast a magical, luminous glow over the ceremony tomorrow evening. Thyme had outdone herself, I thought. Between the lights and the mason jars filled with flowers, the backyard would look charming and inviting, in that tumbledown, beachside way it had. It was the perfect setting.

I inhaled the sea air and wondered what the hold up was. The rehearsal should have started ten minutes ago. While I waited, I ticked through my mental to-do list:

Wedding rehearsal.

Luncheon.

Final fitting.

Harvest herbs and flowers from the garden for wedding cake.

Bake, fill, and frost the cake.

Swing through the tent to make sure everything's set for tomorrow.

Then, when I was done, I planned to reward myself with a long hot soak in the scented bath salts Sage had left in my room. I'd picked my suite especially for the deep soaking tub with a view of the grounds and the ocean. I could almost feel my shoulders sinking into the warm bath water.

The sight of a figure out on the dunes interrupted my daydreaming. Someone was roaming around on our private beach.

I squinted into the late morning sun and frowned. The shape was a man. For a few seconds, I thought he might be one-half of the birding enthusiast couple, but then I noticed his business suit. It seemed unlikely that a bird watcher would be out on the beach in a suit. Frankly, it seemed weird for anyone to choose business attire for a walk along the shore. What was he doing out there?

Before I could come up with a plausible explanation, Sage and Thyme materialized beside me.

They'd been talking to Marie, our childhood piano teacher, who was also an accomplished harpist. No doubt they were hammering out some last-minute music decision. I'd left the music up to Dave and my sisters to work out.

"You all set?" Sage asked, her voice quavering with emotion.

In answer, I smiled and hooked one of my arms through her elbow and the other through Thyme's. Not only were my sisters my maids of honor, they were also my escorts for the trip down the aisle. I'd have been fine to make the walk alone, but they'd insisted.

Marie plucked her opening chords and the three of us stepped forward onto the path. It was a warm day, but the salted breeze coming up from the ocean was cool and refreshing.

We reached the gazebo, covered with wildflowers out of deference to Thyme's fierce floral allergy. Dave stood beneath the canopy of wisteria, trillium, and violets and grinned at me. Sage and Thyme fell back a step and I placed my hand on Dave's arm, almost not believing that in a day and a half he'd be my husband.

He kissed my cheek and whispered, "What are you thinking?"

"I'm thinking you smell like grouper," I whispered back.

It was true. I was also still thinking about the stranger on the beach. He seemed out of place and oddly menacing.

Beside me, Dave tried to choke back his laughter at my crack about him smelling fishy. He failed miserably and ended up sputtering loudly.

Reverend Mark, Dave's childhood friend, who'd flown in from his church in Michigan to officiate our ceremony, gave us both a stern look. I'd only met Mark a handful of times, but I knew him well enough to know the disapproval was mostly for show. After all, this was the man who'd left a whoopee cushion on my chair at Christmas dinner with the entire Drummond family. He was the perfect person to join us in matrimony.

Mark cleared his throat and began to walk us through how the ceremony would go. I resisted the urge to turn around and scan the beach behind us. Dave grabbed my hand and held it tightly while Mark talked. I smiled into his brown eyes.

I tried to put the man on the beach out of my

mind and shake off the cloud of worry threatening to settle around my shoulders. He was nobody.

Unless, of course, he was somebody—somebody sent by the Atlantic City loan shark who had a grudge against my parents; somebody sent by Alayna, the sociopath who'd killed one of my clients and had tried to pin it on me; somebody connected to one of the dozens of killers Dave had brought to justice during his years as a homicide detective.

Stop it, I told myself. Herk the Jerk is out of the picture. Alayna is in a women's prison near Sacramento. And you are literally thousands of miles away from the LAPD and its cast of criminals. That guy is just some random weirdo looking for shells. There's nothing ominous about him.

It might have been easier to dismiss him if both of my sisters hadn't also had recent brushes with the criminal underbelly of society. What if he was connected to the blackmailing scandal that had unfolded at the golf club where Roman and Sage's boss was a member? Or what if he was connected to Victor's sister's ex-husband, who was, by all reports, a violent—scratch that, murderous— corrupt ex-police officer. Heck, among the three of us, Sage, Thyme, and I had probably had enough mortal enemies to fill one entire table at the reception.

I rolled my shoulders and forced myself to focus on what Reverend Mark was saying. I could feel Dave's eyes on me, curious and worried. So I jutted out my hip and gave him a playful bump. The anxiety melted from his face and he shook his head in good-natured amusement.

"Then you'll say your vows. Blah, blah, blah. And kiss the bride," Mark said.

"Blah, blah, blah?" Sage asked, frowning. "Maybe they should rehearse them."

I shook my head. "No. We wrote our own. I want them to be a surprise."

Now Thyme leaned forward to catch the minister's eyes. "Are you sure that's a good idea, Reverend Mark?"

"No worries. I've had the sneak preview. I can assure you they're heartfelt and wholly appropriate. Rosemary and Dave just want to wait until tomorrow to share them with the rest of the world," he assured my sisters.

"You didn't let her make any jokes in hers, did you?" Thyme stage whispered. "Her jokes are terrible."

"Lousy," Sage confirmed.

"I can *hear* you, you know."

Even though I came right back at them with a retort of my own, I was glad for my sisters' gentle teasing. I almost forgot about the man lurking on the beach. Almost, but not quite.

As Mark shook his head and tried to move on, I couldn't help craning my neck to scan the shoreline out of the corner of my eye.

The beach was deserted. Now, I found myself wondering where the stranger had gone.

CHAPTER 8

SAGE

I watched Chelle pull the fabric tight around Rosemary's back. She muttered to herself around the pins in her mouth. Thyme shot me a worried look. Meanwhile, the bride-to-be seemed to be oblivious to the tension in the room.

"Can you alter it in time for tomorrow?" I asked the seamstress.

Chelle exhaled, her breath ruffling her long bangs, and removed the pins before answering. "I can. But you and your sister make sure Miss Wasting Away here eats between now and then, would you? Otherwise, she's going to be lost in this thing no matter what I do."

She stepped back and examined her handiwork. Luckily, Rosemary hadn't chosen a particularly floofy dress. I mean, it's not as though there were yards and yards of satin and miles of lace enveloping her. She didn't even have a train. So with the streamlined cut, I was pretty confident Chelle could work her magic.

Rosemary twirled and examined herself in the mirror. She must've liked what she saw because she reached over and squeezed the seamstress. "Thank you so much, Chelle. It means a lot to me that you're doing my dress."

Another glance from Thyme.

Chelle and our mom had been good friends before our parents had gone off on their late-in-life adventure—or, as Rosemary would put it, before they fled the jurisdiction. I suppose the truth is they *were* closer to fugitives from justice than happy-go-lucky retirees. But, I tried not to think about it that way.

Chelle must've heard some deeper meaning in Rosemary's words, too. Chelle squeezed her before holding her at arms-length and giving her a good, long look. "Your mama would be so proud of you," she sniffled softly. She glanced over Rosemary's head and swept Thyme and me into her gaze. "She'd be proud of all three of you. I just wish she could be here to see this."

The guest room Rosemary had claimed as her bridal suite was utterly quiet. Thyme nodded with an appropriately mournful look. Rosemary quirked her mouth.

Before she could say anything snarky, I hurried to fill the silence. "Rosemary said you can't you make it to the wedding tomorrow. We'll miss you, but we're glad you were able to join us for the luncheon."

She dabbed her eyes. "I'm sorry I'll miss it, too. But ... some dear friends have come into town unexpectedly, and I haven't seen them in quite some time." Chelle was clearly fumbling around for an excuse.

Now I felt guilty. I hadn't meant to put her on the spot.

Thyme rescued both of us. "How wonderful that you're going to have an opportunity to reconnect with old friends! Isn't that the *best*?"

Rosemary stepped out of the gown, and we eased it into the big white garment bag that Dave insisted on calling a body bag. I figured he ought to know what a body bag looked like, what with being a homicide detective and all. I'd overheard Rosemary tell him if he peeked inside this one, he'd need a real one.

As Chelle zipped the bag closed, she gave Rosemary a final warning. "I mean it about not losing any more weight. Brides and crash diets don't mix. I ought to know."

"What do you mean?" Rosemary asked.

"Well, I worked with a bride once who dropped a ton of weight the week of her wedding but didn't come see me for adjustments. As she and her new husband were walking down the aisle to leave the church, her strapless dress went *zoop!*" Chelle gestured dramatically, flinging her arms down the sides of her body toward the floor. "There it lay, on the floor of the church, puddled around her feet."

"Oh, yikes." I cringed for the unnamed, undressed bride.

"That wasn't the worst of it; she wasn't wearing anything underneath. Didn't want to ruin the line."

Thyme's mouth popped open and her eyes grew round.

Rosemary giggled. "I guess that's one way to have a day to remember."

"That must've been the most embarrassing wedding ceremony in recorded history," I mused.

You'd think so," the seamstress said, warming to the subject. "But at least Lady Godiva's ceremony ended with a marriage, unlike another wedding I attended. At that one, the priest asked the groom, 'Do you take this woman?' The groom thought about it for a bit then answered, 'You know, I'm really not sure.'"

We were silent for a long moment, imagining the scene.

Chelle continued, "I always thought it would have been a kindness if that man had just not shown up. Better to be left standing at the altar by somebody who got cold feet than to be rejected in front of your friends and family."

Rosemary tilted her head. Her expression was thoughtful, as if she were considering the pros and cons of both approaches.

"I'm going to go back to the shop right now and whip through these alterations," Chelle promised. She nodded in Thyme's direction, "If you want to come with me, you can wait and bring the dress back."

I tried to suppress a frown. I was in charge of the dresses. Thyme was in charge of the flowers, the music, and the place settings. I didn't like the idea of Thyme traipsing off with Chelle without me.

But I could hear my father's voice in my head, chiding me: *'Oh, Sage, you don't **have** to have middle-child syndrome if you don't want to.'* So I managed a tight smile.

"Sure, as long as that works for Thyme's schedule. You didn't have plans with Victor, did you?"

"Nope. I'm happy to run into town," she chirped. She guided Chelle toward the door with one hand, the dress bag folded over her other forearm.

I glanced over at Rosemary after the door closed behind them. She was looking out the window toward the ocean, but something about her gaze made me think her mind wasn't on the whitecaps.

"Everything okay?" I asked.

After a beat, she turned toward me. "Just thinking."

"About your dress falling off or about Dave equivocating during the vows?" I teased.

She chuckled, but I thought her laugh sounded oddly hollow. And I couldn't help noticing she didn't answer my question. For a wild moment, I thought she was going to tell me *she* was having second thoughts about getting married. But she didn't, and I wasn't sure how to broach the topic.

CHAPTER 9

THYME

I wished I'd thought to grab a book to bring along to pass the time while Chelle altered Rosemary's gown. But I hadn't. And Chelle, ordinarily vivacious to a fault, did not like to be distracted when she worked. So she set me up with a mug of chai and several issues of some glossy fashion magazine while she shut herself away in her back room to focus. I flipped halfheartedly through the magazines for a few minutes, but to tell the truth I'm more of a Scientific American or Mental Floss girl. I put the stack of magazines aside and sipped my drink while I occupied myself with one of my favorite pastimes: people watching.

I've never been able to decide if I majored in psychology because I'm so interested in the strange behavior of strangers or if I'm so interested in the behavior of strangers because I majored in psychology. Either way, I found it fascinating to speculate about what was going on with the passersby outside the big picture window in the front of the dress shop.

Take the harried father pushing the double stroller with one hand and holding an armload of grocery bags in the other. Did he know his sweatshirt was on inside out? Where was his partner? I pictured a mom out of town for business while he juggled the kids. Or maybe he was a Mr. Mom and this was all part of his daily routine. Although, judging by the harried expression (and the inside-out shirt) he wore, I was guessing this was not an ordinary Friday afternoon for him.

Then there was the older couple who'd been making out on the wrought-iron bench across the square from the shop for at least the last ten minutes. They appeared to be in their early seventies. She was a petite Asian woman. He was a tall African-American man with silver hair. And they were sucking face like a pair of teenagers. Were they a married couple who'd been together for half a century and still felt the spark of love and lust? Or high school sweethearts who'd been separated by time and circumstance and had only just redis-covered one another after their respective spouses passed away? Or, I thought, warming to this idea, were they star-struck lovers carrying on a decades' long extramarital affair who had traveled to Seashore to spend a weekend together without fear of being caught?

The man must have felt me watching him, because when the couple came up for air, he shifted his gaze toward the window where I sat. I flicked my eyes away quickly, and that's when I saw the man in the suit standing outside the candy shop. He was watching me watch the lovebirds.

As soon as my eyes met his, he turned his atten-tion to The Sugarplum Shoppe's window display. But I wasn't fooled. As a veteran people watcher myself, it was easy for me to tell when I'd busted someone watching me. I laughed to myself and picked up the nearest magazine. I flipped it opened it to a random page then peeked over it to get a better view of my watcher.

He stood out, that much was for sure. One, he was wearing a black business suit and tie in a town where the dress code meant your good pair of flip-flops qualified as formal attire.

Two, he had the squared-off muscular

physique of someone who considered his body to be a temple. He stood, ramrod straight. Square jawed, with his haircut cropped close to his head, he screamed 'military discipline.' There was no way this guy was salivating over dark chocolate fudge drizzled with sea salt caramel or coconut cream cupcakes dotted with crystallized ginger. I'd have placed money on him being one of those extreme fitness dudes who ate almost nothing but meat jerky and dragged trucks around by ropes.

Seashore, New Jersey, was the quintessential beach town, home to a handful of Victorian bed-and-breakfasts, several gift shops specializing in nautical-themed household goods and overpriced children's clothes with anchors embroidered on the pockets. There was a flower shop and a funky little bookstore, a bead shop, and a pet store. There was one hair salon, Curls by Clare, and a barbershop, complete with a red-and-white striped pole. A handful of restaurants, most of them specializing in seafood (with the notable exception of Marcello's Trattoria), two bakeries, a coffee and tea shop, and one consignment store rounded out the main square.

Seashore was not a town that hosted corporate retreats, conferences, or business meetings of any kind. The county courthouse was located in the county seat, two towns over, and even the town solicitor favored Hawaiian shirts and khaki shorts. Maybe, *maybe,* you'd see someone wearing a suit at a funeral, but that was about the extent of it. So, lawyer, banker, or candlestick maker—whoever he was, the guy in front of the candy store didn't blend in.

I spent a few minutes trying to come up with a good story for the guy in the suit, but the best I could manage was that he was an assassin. As if there'd be a paid hit man roaming around this speck of a seaside town, I scoffed at myself. Still, I shivered at my own overactive imagination.

I turned slightly in the chair so I was looking away from him and grabbed one of the magazines. I paged through it listlessly, until Chelle emerged triumphantly from the back room holding the long white bag. Her arm was high above her head to keep the bottom of the bag from dragging along the floor.

I dropped the magazine and shot up. "You're finished already?"

She nodded. "It wasn't hard. I just needed to add some darts and take in the seams in the back."

"Thanks again. You've done a beautiful job

with the dress, and it means a lot to all three of us that you've been involved."

She crossed the sunlit room and handed me the dress bag in an almost formal gesture, sort of bowing from the waist as she did so. "And I mean what I said earlier, Thyme. I wish I could be there tomorrow, but my friends...."

I nodded as she trailed off. "We understand." I leaned in and gave her a peck on the cheek. "The next time the three of us are at the resort, we'll have you out for dinner and we can look through the wedding pictures together."

"I'd like that."

She walked me to the door and held it open as I maneuvered my way through the doorway with my precious cargo. She gave me a little wave goodbye and flipped the sign hanging from the door from 'Open' to "Closed' before going back inside to close up the shop for the day.

For such a simple dress, Rosemary's wedding gown weighed a ton. I staggered toward the resort's old truck with my awkward load, grateful for our little town's ample parking during the off-season.

At least I didn't have far to go, seeing as how I'd snagged a spot close to the dress shop.

I fumbled awkwardly for the keys with my left hand while holding the garment bag up high so it didn't hit the sidewalk. Somehow, I ended up twisted into a modified standing triangle pose, which is how I caught a glimpse of the suit guy out of my peripheral vision as I was unlocking the passenger side door to the truck.

He'd left his post in front of the candy shop, and was now standing across the street in front of the old bank. His back was to me, and he was staring into the front window, which wouldn't have been noteworthy, except for the fact the bank had been shuttered since Sage's freshman year of college.

She'd sent them a resume looking for a summer job. By the time she'd come home for an interview, Atlantic Coast Savings & Loan had been bought by a large New York bank and our little seaside branch was on the chopping block. The bank's closing was a blow to the town, especially to our parents, who ended up securing funding from less savory sources once the bank left town.

In any case, unless the guy in the suit was a big fan of dust, spiders, or yellowing paper, there wasn't really anything inside worth looking at. The thought that he might be following me hit my central nervous system like a shot of espresso, and I shoved the bag with Rosemary's dress onto the passenger seat, no longer worried about keeping it pristine. As I jammed the keys into the ignition my hands were shaking.

I took a centering breath as I started the engine. Don't panic, I ordered myself. Why would some random man be following me?

My effort at reasoning myself out of my worry failed miserably.

Because I could think of tons of reasons why the man in the suit would be following me. Maybe he worked for one of my parents' creditors. As far as we knew, the bank—a real bank—now held all their outstanding debt, and we'd made a ton of progress in paying it down. So much so, that they'd actually forgiven part of it and had extended the deadline to make the final balloon payment. But that hadn't stopped Herk the Jerk from continuing to try to get a piece of the action. He believed he'd been cut out and wasn't happy about it, to put it mildly. Perhaps he'd found some small, overlooked debt our parents owed to some other loan shark and was back in the picture.

Or maybe this guy lurking around the bank had some connection to Helena, Victor's sister. Her abusive ex-husband had been a crooked police officer in Brazil and had stalked her to New York. He was behind bars now, but seeing as how I was instrumental in putting him there, he could conceivably be nursing a grudge.

My trembling worsened, and the truck lurched as I drove along the quaint streets that led from the square to the road out to the beach. Despite the bright, sunny afternoon, my mind had gone to a dark, frightened place, and I couldn't seem to bring it back. I sped out of town and, without signaling, made a sharp right at speed onto the bumpy access road that curved through Clyde and Lila Dowell's farm. It wasn't technically a public road, but I'd worked for the Dowells for four summers, and I had a standing invitation to take the shortcut home from town.

Of course, that invitation would not extend to suit-wearing outsiders. I could almost picture Lila standing on the wide-beamed porch, in a sundress and barefoot, shouldering Clyde's hunting rifle as she shot out my pursuer's tires. I surprised myself by giggling at the image. Then I checked my rearview mirror. Nothing behind me but dusty road.

I let out a big *whoosh* of breath and removed my tense hands, one at a time, from the steering wheel to shake them out before my muscles cramped.

Maybe that guy was a real estate broker in town to see the bank building. Or a commercial appraiser or something. And maybe he had a wicked sweet tooth, so he was salivating over The Sugarplum's treats. The explanations I created seemed flimsy even to me, but with each mile I put between myself and town, I believed them more.

I zipped along the access road until it dumped the truck out onto the gravel ribbon that led to the back of the resort. My heart rate had slowed almost to normal, although I couldn't stop myself from looking behind me every few seconds to confirm I was alone.

But by the time I'd parked the truck and gathered up the dress to deliver it to Rosemary's room, I had almost convinced myself that the entire situation had been a figment of my imagination.

CHAPTER 10

ROSEMARY

*S*age had hung around in my room after Thyme left with Chelle and my dress. I could tell she wanted to have a heart-to-heart, but I was too distracted for a sisterly sit down. I assumed she wanted to talk about my upcoming transition from single to married or some similarly sentimental subject. Her endearing mushiness is what made Sage Sage, but I didn't have time for mush—not until I managed to whittle down my to-do list. By a lot.

So, after a bit, I suggested she go check on our aunts, uncles, and cousins who'd made the trip in for the wedding while I got started on my cake. Sage, being Sage, instantly offered to help me gather the ingredients and make the batter, but I told her that baking as meditation only works when the baker is alone. She understood and set off to find our Aunt Ruby.

I headed to the mudroom off the kitchen to borrow a pair of gardening gloves, shears, and a basket from the racks by the door. Then I followed the stone path outside the door as it wound through the grounds, past the vegetable gardens on the left and the riotous flower gardens on the right. At the stone bench my dad had installed in honor of my mother's fiftieth birthday, I made a big loop behind the labyrinth where guests could experience walking meditation. On the other side of the maze, I ducked under a canopy of overgrown tree branches and entered the herb garden.

My plan was to gather the lavender and any of the other aromatic herbs that looked appealing then stop by the flower gardens to snip some honeysuckle on my way back to the kitchen. The decorative flowers for the cake topper would have to wait until later in the afternoon when the sun wasn't so high. I didn't want them to wilt before I had a chance to crystallize them.

I crouched beside the lavender plants. For this early in the season, the sun beat hot on the back of my neck. The only sounds were of birds singing and the rhythmic snip of my shears cutting through the herbs. Once I filled my basket, I stood to leave.

But, my feet had plans of their own, and I found myself detouring to the far corner of the garden, right at the crest of the hill, where my parents had planted the namesake plot—rosemary, sage, parsley, and thyme stood in tidy concentric circles surrounded by a round, white fence. I rested my basket under a tree and leaned against the trunks, smiling as the childhood memories came rushing back like water over rocks.

I remembered the game of garden tag Sage, Thyme, and I had created one summer. The rules constantly evolved, becoming increasingly complex as the weeks wore on. But, somehow, whenever the children of guests happened to turn up in the garden, the visitors seamlessly slipped into the game, changing it yet again in the process.

I laughed softly to myself. I don't often indulge in walks down memory lane. And, after the way the three of us came to own the resort, I tried hard not to think about my parents at all. But I guess the day before a girl's wedding was as good a time as any for a bout of nostalgia. My eyes swam with tears—at what, I wasn't sure. But I turned away from the garden and stared out over the horizon until the sadness passed.

After a while, I picked up my basket and turned to leave. That's when I saw two sets of sunglass-shrouded eyes staring at me from deep within the thicket of bushes to my right. I gasped and almost dropped the basket.

The people who'd been watching me turned and raced down the hill toward the beach. I chased them halfheartedly for several yards, calling after them to wait. I realized that was probably not the safest response to being stalked, but I wanted to find out who they were and why they'd been crouching in my bushes.

As the pair curved right to follow the shoreline, my eyes focused on their floppy, wide-brimmed hats. I realized they'd both had pairs of binoculars hanging around their necks. When I put that information together with the matching khaki vests and shorts they were wearing, I realized I must have startled the bird-watching Simons. Oddly enough, Parsley, our family cat, was trotting along behind them. He generally gave strangers a wide berth, but I suppose he figured they'd lead him to a delectable feathered snack.

I felt moderately bad about startling them, but

they'd certainly reacted oddly to having stumbled across someone in their hunt for blackbirds and thrushes. I didn't have time to track them down and apologize. I had a wedding cake to bake. I changed course and cut across the lawn in a diagonal, stopping to pick some honeysuckles before going back to the kitchen.

But when I entered the kitchen, Thyme was leaning against the big commercial refrigerator, tapping her foot.

"There you are. Chelle finished your dress. Let's go back to your room so you can try it on."

I dropped the basket on the counter. "I really need to get this cake batter started," I stalled.

Thyme fixed me with a look. "Rosemary, we have to make sure it fits. If you come try it on now, I promise I'll help you with your batter."

I couldn't stifle my laugh. First Sage, and now Thyme. It was sweet that they wanted to help me bake this cake. But the last time I checked, their kitchen skills were firmly in the peanut butter and jelly sandwich and takeout menu category. I wrapped a clean dishcloth around the lavender and honeysuckle flowers and stuck the bundle in the refrigerator.

"Okay, I'll try on the dress, but then I want you

guys to promise to leave me alone till I get this blasted cake in the oven."

She beamed at me. "It's a deal."

Then she pulled me through the door like a kid excited to go find Christmas presents under the tree. Correction: the way I imagine a kid excited to find Christmas presents under her tree would act. MJ and Bart Field didn't celebrate Christmas. Or Hanukkah. And the winter equinox was generally not a time of gift giving. Thinking about my parents reminded me of the herb garden.

"I was harvesting my lavender and I ran into that couple, the Simons."

"Did you talk to them?"

"No, and it was kind of weird, actually. They were in the bushes—looking for birds, I guess. When I spotted them, they took off running for the beach. We should ask Kay to tell them they don't have to hide. They just can't crash the wedding."

Thyme nodded. "I'll let her know."

As we reached the door to my room, I mused, "I just hope they don't run into that weird guy on the beach."

"What weird guy?"

I waved my hand. "Never mind; it's a long story."

Thyme pursed her lips and waited.

"There was some man down on the beach this morning while we were having the rehearsal," I said.

"He could have been a jogger who got lost and ended up on our private beach. It happens all the time."

She was right that it happened all the time. But the man in the suit was no runner who'd gone off course. I just shrugged. "Maybe. It doesn't matter."

I dug into my pocket for the key to my room, but Thyme put her hand on my arm. "You left it unlocked. That's how I got in with the dress."

I blinked at her. "Did I really?"

"You must have." She studied me closely but didn't say anything further.

I could have sworn I'd locked the door. I turned the knob and, sure enough, the door swung open. She trailed me into the room.

She'd hung the dress on the vintage wire dress form standing between the mirror in the corner and the French doors that opened directly out onto a small patio overlooking the grounds. As it did every time I saw it, the gown took my breath away. I only hoped it would have the same effect on

Dave. I shrugged out of my sundress and Thyme zipped me into my wedding dress.

I smoothed my hands along the delicate overlay of lace. It definitely fit more snuggly than it had just a few hours earlier. I didn't think I'd have to worry about standing in my underpants in front of all of our guests tomorrow. I did a little turn to admire myself in the mirror.

"You're luminous," Thyme said in a hushed voice.

I met her eyes in the mirror. "I think you mean sweaty. It was hot out in the garden."

She giggled, then held up a hand. "I know you want to get back to your cake. Let me just go find Sage so she can see you in the dress before you take it off. We don't want her to feel left out."

As much as I did want to get back to the kitchen, I knew Thyme was right. If Sage found out Thyme had seen me in the altered dress and she hadn't, her feelings *would* be hurt.

"Okay," I agreed "but make it snappy. I really need to get my cakes in the oven."

She nodded and ran out the door.

CHAPTER 11

SAGE

I was putting the finishing touches on the wedding favors when Thyme burst into the parlor, out of breath and red-faced.

"Do you ever just walk into a room anymore?" I asked mildly curious, as I cut lengths of pale blue satin ribbon to exactly eighteen inches.

"It doesn't seem like it," she admitted. "But I'm in a hurry for a reason this time. Do you want to see Rosemary in her dress?"

I placed the scissors and the ribbon on the table and stood. "Sure. These can wait." I waved my hand over the table.

The three of us had spent a weekend last month making jars of rosemary sea salt and bottling tiny tubes of tupelo honey—a nod to Rosemary and

Dave's childhood homes, her name, and their personalities—a little bit salty, a little bit sweet. The favors were cute, personal, and would be yummy, if I did say so myself. And, perhaps most important of all, because we made them ourselves, they'd turned out to be fairly inexpensive. And Rosemary and Dave were stretching every dime in their budget as far as it would go.

Thyme said, "She looks gorgeous. And she wants you to see her in it. But we have to hurry so she can get started on her cakes."

My eyes widened. "Get *started?* What's she been doing all afternoon?"

She shook her head as we headed toward Rosemary's room. "I know, it seems like she should be further along than she is. She did get the herbs from the garden. Oh, and I guess she ran into those bird watchers while she was out there," she added casually.

My heart skipped a beat and my mind started to race. "She met the Simons?" I asked, trying to keep my voice level.

"I wouldn't say she met them, exactly. She spotted them in the bushes, and they ran away. I think Kay might've scared them into thinking they're not allowed to be out and about in public at all this weekend. I told Rosemary I'd talk to Kay about it," she assured me.

I found my voice and said, "No! I'll do it."

Thyme gave me a strange look—probably because my tone had been so sharp.

I blew out a long breath and tried again. "I mean, I know you're busy with the decorations. I'll take care of it for you."

"However you want to do it," she murmured.

I rapped softly on Rosemary's door.

There was no answer.

"Rosemary?" I called after moment.

Still no answer. We looked at each other. Then Thyme shrugged and turned the doorknob.

"Rosemary, are you decent?" she asked as she opened the door, and we stepped inside.

The empty garment bag lay draped over the back of the Queen Anne chair near the window. Rosemary's sundress and shoes were in a tidy pile on the floor beside the mirror. But Rosemary and the wedding gown were nowhere to be seen.

The French doors that opened to the patio were ajar. A chill crept up my spine, but I kept my voice steady. "She's probably in the bathroom."

Thyme's face was drawn, but she nodded gamely. "Right, the bathroom."

We stood in silence for half a minute, waiting for Rosemary to come out of the bathroom even though we both knew she wasn't in there. After a bit, Thyme pushed the bathroom door open and stuck her head into the room.

"She's not in there," Thyme informed me unnecessarily.

"Maybe she decided to go back to the kitchen —" I began lamely.

"Wearing her wedding dress?" Thyme countered.

I shrugged, but she was right. Rosemary would have changed her clothes first. And put on her shoes, I thought, looking down at the sandals by the chair. Everything about this picture was wrong.

Thyme walked over to the French doors. "And why are these doors open?" She pulled them shut with a sharp click.

"Maybe she decided she needed more lavender and took the shortcut across the lawn. Or maybe she just wanted some fresh air and forgot to close them before she went ... wherever she went. I don't know, but I'm sure there's a reasonable explanation."

Thyme lowered herself into the chair and leaned back against the garment bag. She closed her eyes for a brief moment before meeting my eyes. "I'm not so sure. I thought someone might have been following me when I was in town. A guy in a suit. It really kind of freaked me out."

"A guy in a suit? Do you mean a business suit?"

She nodded. "Right. He clearly didn't belong in Seashore. He stood outside the candy shop the entire time I was waiting for Chelle to make the alterations. Then, when I left, he was across the street pretending to look into the old bank building. But he was watching me." Her voice shook.

I crossed the floor and put my arm around her narrow, trembling shoulders. "Do you think he followed you here?" I asked gently.

She tried to catch her breath. "I don't know. I took the shortcut through the Dowells' farm. And I didn't see anyone behind me. But I got a bad vibe from the whole thing. And now Rosemary is missing."

"She's not missing. She's just not here." Even as I said it, I fully realized how stupid it sounded.

Thyme ignored my statement entirely. "And she said there was some weirdo wandering around down on the beach earlier today."

She said it under her breath, more to herself than to me, but I latched onto it.

"What kind of weirdo on the beach?"

"I don't know. She didn't want to talk about it. But it obviously bothered her because she was worried the bird watchers might run into him."

I pursed my lips and thought, trying to make sense of it. "You don't think she ... changed her mind, do you?"

"About getting married? No way," Thyme insisted. "Not Rosemary. No, Sage, something bad happened. I can feel it."

My heart sank. I sort of hoped she'd just taken off to clear her head, but I had to agree with Thyme. Rosemary's disappearance seemed ominous—not to mention out of character. "Yeah, me, too," I admitted.

"Should we call the police? Or tell somebody? Organize a search of the grounds?"

I took a few seconds to consider what I was about to do, but I really didn't have any other choice. "Not yet. Come with me."

I took her by the elbow and led her to the door. I turned the knob, pushed the door open, and came face-to-face with Rosemary's fiancé.

CHAPTER 12

THYME

I reached behind my back and pulled the door to Rosemary's room shut with a sharp bang. Then I pasted a smile on my face.

"Hi, Dave," I chirped.

I risked a glance at Sage. She'd gone wide-eyed and pale. I wasn't surprised.

Of the three of us, she was the worst liar. And, of the three of us, I was the best. I've always chalked it up to being the youngest and having the most vivid imagination. Whatever the cause, my ability to spin whoppers was about to come in handy. I leaned back against the door and tried to look casual.

"Hi, Sage. Hi, Thyme," Dave said.

He waited for me to move.

I didn't budge.

"I'm just going to see if Rosemary wants to take a walk." He jerked his head to the side as if to say 'so, kindly move it.'

"You can't see her right now," I told him.

He narrowed his eyes. "Oh, I can't? Who's going to stop me?" he asked in a voice that made clear he was mostly, but not entirely, joking.

Beside me, Sage was still mute.

"We are. You can't go in there because she's wearing her wedding dress."

His eyes filled with comprehension. "Really?"

"Yep." As far as I knew, it was the truth.

That's the thing about a good lie: it always contains a kernel of truth. If your lie is built on the truth, even a rookie like Sage could keep the ball rolling.

"Why?" he asked.

Sage chimed in, "It was a little loose, so Chelle did some last-minute alterations so it'll fit like a glove tomorrow."

I felt a bizarre flush of pride at how well she'd handled the question.

Dave nodded. "Okay, thanks for warning me. I'll just give her a few minutes to get decent and then I'll—"

I grabbed him by the arm and said, "You'll have to see her later. She actually just sent us to come find you. We need you to help us with something."

I guided him away from the room while I searched my mind for a task to occupy him with while we tracked down his missing bride.

"We were? I mean, we were!" Sage said.

I quickened my pace but tried not to make it obvious that I was hustling him away from the door. In a flash of brilliance, I steered him through the hall back to the parlor where I'd been working on the favors.

"Here's the thing," I told him. "Sage and I have to take care of something with Kay. So, Rosemary thought you could lend us a hand and finish packaging up these gift bags."

Dave made a skeptical face. "Really? She said she wants me to do this?"

Sage nodded.

"She sure does," I chirped enthusiastically.

"She hasn't wanted me to touch anything. I'm afraid I won't do it to her specifications," he worried.

It was a legitimate concern. Rosemary could be ... exacting. But this was no time to get hung up on perfection. We needed to keep him busy. And, from a realistic standpoint, the favors weren't going to package themselves while Sage and I were running around looking for the missing bride.

Sage was tapping on her cell phone. "I'm telling Roman to find Victor and come down here to help you," she said.

"Have them bring a bucket of beers, too," I suggested, sweetening the pot.

Dave nodded, considering. "Okay, I guess it won't be too bad if I have company and some cold ones."

I smiled and gave him an encouraging pat on the arm. "You'll finish in no time. Just make sure you cut those ribbons to exactly eighteen inches ... or else."

We shared a chuckle at Rosemary's expense.

Dave had brightened considerably by now. "Will do. Will the three of you come join us when you're done doing whatever it is you have to do?"

"Definitely," I promised. "We can play cards or something until dinner."

Sage inclined her head toward the door. "We should get going."

I suspected she didn't want to have to attempt lying to Roman's face. And I didn't want her to.

He'd be able to tell in a heartbeat that she was spinning a tale.

We waved goodbye to Dave, who was inspecting the fabric shears as if they might be some sort of illegal contraband, and darted into the hall.

I waited until we'd rounded the corner toward the main hall to speak. "Okay, I bought us some time. Now what's your brilliant idea?"

She pressed her lips together in a worried line. Then she said, "You said she ran into the Simons, right?"

"Right. So?"

"So, if they're out wandering around the grounds, they may have seen or heard something."

"I guess it's possible," I said flatly, unable to muster any real enthusiasm for this plan.

Unless a hawk had carried off our sister, I thought it was unlikely the bird watchers would be much help. But, seeing as how I didn't have any better ideas, I kept my opinion to myself.

We cut through the reception area on our way to the cottages on the other side of the property. Kay looked up from a phone call and gave us a little nod of greeting.

Sage had her head down and was striding

purposely through the lobby. I wouldn't say she seemed eager to get to the Simons' cottage, though. In fact, she seemed more nervous now than she was when we were busy lying our butts off to a trained law enforcement professional just minutes ago. She didn't talk as we left the main house and followed the path around to the back where the individual cottages were situated.

Her silence gave me time to wonder whether we'd made a mistake by keeping Rosemary's disappearance from Dave. After all, he was a detective. He would probably be able to help us find her.

But I didn't want him to think she'd gotten cold feet and bolted. I was sure she wasn't having second thoughts about getting married. Well, I was reasonably sure. I couldn't help but remember how she'd reacted to Chelle's story about the equivocating groom.

We reached the walkway to the front door of the middle of the three cottages, the one we called the Rose Cottage. Sage stopped by the wild rose bushes as if she were steeling herself for battle.

"Why are you being so weird? Just knock on the door and ask them if they saw anything," I told her.

She sighed, stepped up to the door, and raised

her hand to rap on it. Just then, I heard a familiar meow.

I turned in the direction of the sound and saw Parsley, the family cat. Our parents had left him in Kay's care because even they must have realized a cat and the open ocean isn't a match made in heaven. But I was surprised to see him sitting on the windowsill inside the cottage we'd rented to the Simons. As a rule, he wasn't overly friendly with strangers.

"Parsley, what are you doing in there?" I asked.

The cat mewed in response and butted his head against the window screen.

Sage gave the door three quick raps. There was no movement inside, and nobody came to the door.

Parsley clawed at the window screen, his mews morphing into a strangled cry. He wanted to come out.

I hated to invade our guests' privacy, but Parsley had a bit of a destructive streak. I couldn't leave him in there to tear the Simons' belongings to shreds out of boredom.

So I stood in the flowerbed and pushed on the window screen. It popped right out of the frame, just as I'd known it would. The cottage windows were on our long list of deferred maintenance issues to be addressed when we had the cash.

Parsley crawled through the opening and jumped to the ground. He wound himself around my ankles and gave me a short, ticklish lick of thanks before prancing down the path back to the main house and his food bowl.

Sage stuck her head through the open window and craned her neck, looking around the room.

"Mr. Simon? Mrs. Simon?" she called loudly.

"They aren't in there, Sage," I told her, stating the obvious.

She sighed and picked up the screen. I helped her jiggle it back into place.

"Now what?" I said.

She shook her head. "I'm fresh out of ideas."

"Well, I have one," I told her.

"What?"

"We need to call the police."

"We can't."

CHAPTER 13

ROSEMARY

*A*s I prowled around the inside of the storage container like a caged feline trying to burn off excess energy, I took stock of my situation.

In the plus column: the container seemed to be climate-controlled; someone had stuck up a couple of those battery-operated lights people use in their closets, so it wasn't totally dark; and, based on my rough estimate, the space was somewhere between one hundred fifty and two hundred square feet—so, not much smaller than Thyme's expensive apartment in New York.

In the minus column: I had been abducted, which was a pretty significant drawback; I was barefoot and wearing my wedding gown; there was no food, water, or access to a bathroom; and I had no phone, keys, weapon, or anything else that might prove useful if I managed to get out of here. Wherever here was.

So, it was safe to say the bad outweighed the good.

The abduction had happened so fast. I'd been standing around in the suite, waiting for Thyme to return with Sage so I could model the dress, when I'd heard a loud, rustling noise.

It sounded as if it was coming from the wild blueberry thicket just beyond the end of the small patio. At first, I assumed the bird-watching Simons were out traipsing through the trees and shrubs again, but when I peered through the French doors, I caught a glimpse of black.

I stared hard at the black blob, and waited for it to move. After a few seconds, it did, and, through the branches, I spotted a man in a black suit. I was sure he was the man who'd been on the beach earlier.

I flung open the French doors leading out to the patio and darted outside. My heart was racing, but I had had enough. Whoever this guy was, he needed to get lost before my wedding tomorrow. I walked on my toes to the edge of the patio, holding the skirt of my dress up with both hands, like a princess in a movie.

"Hey, you," I shouted.

The guy wheeled around, and we locked eyes. Then he turned back and dived into the bushes.

I was mad, but I wasn't crazy, so I didn't follow him. Instead, I turned back to my room still shaking with adrenaline to wait for my sisters. But I never made it back inside.

Rough, strong hands grabbed me around my waist and pulled me off to the left through an opening in the wild rose bushes. I started to scream, and one beefy forearm encircled my midriff while the other hand clasped hard over my mouth. I thrashed and twisted, trying to get a look at my assailant, but failed. His movements were quick and clean. Professional. As if this probably wasn't his first kidnapping.

He tossed me unceremoniously into the back of a white panel van and locked the doors. I could hear him rattling the handle to make sure the doors were secure before he got in the cab and started the engine. For a moment, I tried to convince myself I was the victim of a surprise bachelorette party, not an abduction. But my sisters knew better than to manufacture a stunt like this. I had a to-do list a mile long.

Of all the ways I'd contemplated spending my last night as a single woman, as a captive in the back of a van hadn't been on the list. The van bumped along. I considered banging my feet and fists against the side, but it would be a fruitless waste of energy. Judging by the unevenness of the road, my attacker was taking the back road out of Tranquility by the Sea along an infrequently traveled, one-lane county road. There'd be no one to hear me if I kicked up a fuss. I slumped against the wall to conserve my energy and plot my next move. This guy had better think again if he thought he was going to prevent me from becoming Mrs. David Drummond tomorrow. But who would want to do such a thing?

I wracked my brain but came up with no answers. We must have driven for about forty minutes before the van lurched to an abrupt stop. The sudden force jerked me back, and I cracked my head against the side panel. As I rubbed the tender spot, I heard a loud creaking. It sounded as if a gate in need of oiling was being raised. I strained to listen over the sound of the idling engine, but I didn't hear voices.

The van inched forward, slowly now. A few moments later, it swung in a wide half circle and reversed. Then we came to a complete stop. The engine cut off. I heard the slam of the door from the passenger cab. I scooted forward and stood, in a low crouch, waiting for the doors to open. I didn't have much of a plan beyond jumping out and running for the hills as soon as I hit the ground, but even that turned out to be undoable.

After some banging and muttered cursing on the other side, the doors swung open and the late afternoon sunlight flooded the darkened interior of the cargo hold. My eyes watered and I blinked rapidly, missing any opening I might've had. When my eyes adjusted, the sight of a large, loutish man with a shaved head holding a baseball bat in his right hand and slapping it into the palm of his left hand was enough to persuade me not to make any attempts to flee. It also drove away any remaining hopes that he was a stripper getting ready to break into a routine.

I trained my eyes on the bat and tried to steady my voice. "Who are you? What do you want?"

He shook his head. It was impossible to tell if he couldn't answer, didn't want to answer, or didn't understand the question. He grunted and gestured for me to get out of the van. I exited and scanned my surroundings. We were in some sort of storage facility. Rows of storage pods stretched out in every direction as far as I could see. He pointed with the bat to an open storage container about four feet in front of me.

I swung my eyes from the large box back to his face. "You don't think I'm getting in there, do you?"

By way of answer, he smacked the bat into his hand again.

My stomach dropped and my knees threatened to buckle.

"I'll take that as a yes," I muttered, reluctantly shuffling forward. The sharp rocks and gravel cut into my bare feet as I trudged toward the storage container. When I got close to the unit, my new friend gave me a rough push forward. I stumbled inside and he rolled down the metal door. I heard the snick of a padlock clicking into place. Then, silence.

The silence stretched on and on. I was glad to have the lights, because being trapped in the space in total darkness would have been unbearable. But, as it was, I was edging closer and closer to hysteria. With each minute that passed, my breathing grew more shallow and rapid. I did *not* want to live out my days in my wedding dress trapped in this pod like some horrible, modern Miss Havisham.

I closed my eyes and tried to meditate my way to calmness. Or at least a state of lesser panic. I sat crossed-legged on the floor and focused on my breathing until I heard footsteps crunching along the gravel, the babble of voices, and the unmistakable grunt of my not-overly loquacious abductor.

My heart thumped with anticipation and I hurried to my feet. The padlock clanged open, and the metal door rolled up.

The bald man tossed an armload of bottled water into the pod. Water bottles rolled around my feet. I snatched one up and took long, greedy swigs of lukewarm water. The man herded two people toward me. A man and a woman. Both wearing khaki vests, knee-length hiking shorts, and floppy hats. A pair of binoculars hung from around the man's neck; a thirty-five-millimeter camera from around the woman's. I recognized them as Mr. and Mrs. Simon from the resort. I couldn't imagine why they were here, but I wasn't going to complain about having some company.

As they shuffled into the pod, I took a closer look at their faces and a jolt of shock tore through me. The water bottle fell to the floor with a dull thud, and I stared, open-mouthed, certain for a moment that I was hallucinating. But, no, I wasn't seeing things.

"No. Oh, hell, no. Listen, you can't put them in here with me. Please." I begged the mute giant standing just outside the storage unit.

He stared at me blankly for a second. Then he rolled down the door and replaced the lock.

Inside, the three of us looked at one another in the shadowy light. My father broke the silence first.

"Hello, Rosemary."

I held his gaze for a moment. "Dad." Then I turned to my mother. "Mom," I said flatly.

Five minutes earlier, I would have said my circumstances were unspeakably bad. I'd have been wrong, though. As bad as it was to be held captive in a storage unit the day before my wedding, it was nothing compared to being held captive in a storage unit the day before my wedding along with my estranged, debt-dodging parents dressed up like bird-watchers.

My mother looked me up and down. "Have you been eating, Rosie?" Her voice held a familiar lilt of nagging concern.

"Now, Mary Jane," my dad warned her.

I dropped my head in my hands and stifled a

groan. Forget Charles Dickens, this was way worse than being a jilted bride wasting away in an attic. This was French existentialism-level bad.

I'd read Sartre's *No Exit* in a French literature class in college—one of the few non-science courses I'd taken. The play and its premise had stayed with me ever since: three damned souls locked in a room together to torture one another in a private hell for all eternity? I'd thought the concept was scarier than the bloodiest of slasher movies.

And now I was living it.

CHAPTER 14

SAGE

*T*hyme stared at me.

After a long silence, she said, "What do you mean, we can't call the police? We have to. The bird watchers aren't around. There are no witnesses. And our sister is missing."

"We can't go to the police because Mr. and Mrs. Simon aren't just a couple of random bird lovers," I began to explain.

"They aren't? Then who are they, Sage?"

I gnawed on my lower lip, trying to decide how best to break the news to her. Unable to come up with a good way to do it, I just blurted it out. "Mom and Dad."

"Mom and Dad?" she echoed faintly.

"I can't believe you didn't figure it out. Simon

had to be the most obvious alias they could have used. I mean, except for Garfunkel, I guess."

Thyme gaped at me in confusion. "I don't understand. What are they doing here?"

"They wanted to see Rosemary get married. They realized they wouldn't be welcome, so they decided to do it from a distance. You know, secretly."

"You helped them, didn't you? You told them about the wedding and had Kay book them a room behind our backs." Her voice was laced with bitterness.

I counted to ten in my head before answering. "Look, we can argue about whether I overstepped or not later. Right now, we need to find Rosemary. And since they were apparently prowling around spying on her, they're our best hope. But we can't go to the police until we know where Mom and Dad are because—"

"Because they'll be arrested if the police stumble over them," she finished.

I exhaled in relief that she understood our predicament. "Exactly."

She pierced me with a long, searching look that made me want to squirm. Then she said in a soft voice, "Rosemary's going to kill you when she finds out."

"That's fine. That'll mean we've found her," I told her, meaning every word of it.

When we hadn't found Rosemary in her room, I'd been sure she'd caught our parents spying on her. I'd painted a detailed, romanticized picture of how it would all unfold: She'd realize the bird watchers were actually Mom and Dad. Once she overcame her initial shock, she'd go back to their cottage so the three of them could talk and put the past behind them.

I imagined them sitting around the small walnut table under the window drinking our mom's iced herbal tea. Our dad would tell corny jokes to break the ice. As Rosemary gradually thawed, Mom would ask her questions about Dave, probing to learn more about the man who'd captured her heart.

And, when Rosemary realized her wedding day wouldn't be the same without our parents, I even hoped she might find a way to forgive them. The fairytale scene had played out, clearly and repeatedly, in my imagination—like a clip from a movie.

Now, though, my optimism seemed, not just

misplaced, but childish. If Rosemary *had* found out the truth about the Simons, I had to admit, she was far more likely to have taken off alone—upset, betrayed, and shaken—than to have indulged in a kumbaya moment with our parents.

But I didn't care how mad she'd be at me. I just wanted to find her. My chest tightened and I pressed my palms against my eyes to keep my tears from escaping.

I was surprised when I felt Thyme wrap her arm around my shoulder. But I couldn't bring myself to meet her eyes.

"It's okay, Sage," she crooned as she rubbed my upper arm gently. "We're going to find her."

I peeked up at her through my wet eyelashes. "I shouldn't have helped them."

"No, you shouldn't have," she agreed.

"I thought ... I thought Rosemary would regret it someday if they weren't here for her wedding."

Thyme's face tightened, but she didn't argue the point. Instead, she pulled me closer and gave me a quick hug. "Your heart's in the right place."

"Thanks," I managed.

She pursed her lips. "Your brain, on the other hand...."

I pulled away. "Hey."

"Sorry," she said, giving me a look that made it clear she wasn't even remotely sorry. She paused for a moment then continued, "We don't have time to hash this all out now."

She was right. I squared my shoulders but couldn't ignore the wave of worry that crashed over me. What had I done?

"Are you sure you're not mad at me?" I asked, unable to stop myself, as we hurried away from the empty cottage and back to the main house.

I knew the fact that our parents were here had been a bombshell for her. I didn't want her to be angry with me.

"No, I'm not mad at you," she said. Before I even had a chance to exhale in relief, she went on, "I'm just ... surprised."

That was understandable. I'm sure she was surprised, stunned—shocked, even—to learn I'd taken it upon myself to let our parents know Rosemary was getting married and then help them sneak onto the resort property so they could watch from a distance.

I flashed her an uncertain smile. "Okay, good. I don't want you to be upset with me."

We walked a few more feet.

Then she said "I'm more hurt, I guess. Why didn't you tell me they were going to be here?"

I stopped in the middle of the path and turned to meet her eyes. "They asked me to keep it a secret, Thyme. They knew Rosemary wouldn't want them here and they didn't want to distract from her day. So Kay, Chelle, and I came up with the bird watching cover story."

As soon as the words were out of my mouth, I realized I'd made a mistake. Now, she was angry— no doubt about it.

"Wait. You told Kay and Chelle? But not me?" she demanded heatedly as her foot tapped rapidly against the stepping stones underfoot.

I tried to reason with her. "I couldn't tell you. I couldn't put you in that position. Imagine if Rosemary found out. It's different with Chelle and Kay, they're Mom's best friends. They love us like daughters, but their loyalties lie with her."

Thyme narrowed her eyes and huffed out a breath. I didn't really want to fight with her. I took a guess that she was primarily upset about being left out.

"It's not just you. I didn't even tell Roman," I said softly.

"Really?"

"Really."

I felt endlessly guilty about that fact, but it seemed to change the dynamic with my younger sister.

Her face softened. "This subject's not closed, Sage. But we need to find Rosemary."

"And Mom and Dad," I added.

As we reached the doors to the lobby, she gave me a dark look but didn't respond.

CHAPTER 15

THYME

Sage and I pushed through the doors to the reception area and clattered across the floor. The sound of our sandals slapping the stone caught Kay's attention.

"Is everything okay, girls?" she asked.

"Not really," Sage told her. "Rosemary's missing."

"Missing? What do you mean?" Kay probed.

"She tried on her gown after Thyme brought it back from Chelle's. Thyme came to get me so I could see it. When we got back to Rosemary's room the French doors were open, and she was gone. She left her shoes, her phone, and her purse behind. As far as we know, she's barefoot and wearing her wedding dress."

"That's bad enough, but when in town, I got the feeling I was being followed," I added. "Something's not right, Kay."

A shadow of worry crossed Kay's tanned face.

"What is it?" I asked softly.

She trained her eyes on Sage and gave a little jerk toward the back office with her head. "I need to talk to you." After a pause, she added, "About the Simons."

"Thyme knows about Mom and Dad," Sage reassured her.

A small sigh of relief leaked out of Kay as if she were a balloon with a pinprick hole. "Good. A little while ago, your parents came running through the lobby doors like the two of you just now. Your mother was beside herself, babbling about an abduction. I couldn't make heads or tails of it."

A fist of ice wrapped itself around my heart. "An abduction? Are you sure that's what she said?"

Kay nodded grimly. "I'm almost positive. Your father stepped in and started talking over her. He said they needed to borrow the old pickup truck. So I got them a set of spare keys."

"I don't suppose you have any idea where they went?" Sage asked in a weak voice.

"I'm sorry, girls. I honestly don't. The only

person who might be able to tell you is Chelle." Kay twisted her hands together into a worried knot.

I shook my head, dismissing the idea. "I was with Chelle most of the afternoon. I doubt she knows what's going on."

"She might," Kay countered. "Chelle's planning to be with them tomorrow—as moral support —while they watch the wedding from that stand of elm trees on the hill. Heaven knows they'll need it. It's going to be hard to watch their baby get married through binoculars. But, anyway, Chelle's one of your mother's closest friends. She might have called her after I gave them the keys."

I tried to ignore my rising anger at her obvious sympathy for my parents. I bit down hard on my lower lip to prevent myself from reminding her that my parents had stiffed her almost three months' salary before they left town. We had paid her back and kept her current even during the resort's leanest times. Just possibly her loyalty was slightly misplaced.

I took a ragged breath, and as Sage looped her elbow through mine, she applied just the slightest pressure to my arm to let me know she understood what I was feeling but that this wasn't the time to get into a big discussion about it. I exhaled slowly. She was right.

"If you hear from either of our parents, call me or Thyme right away," Sage instructed Kay.

"I will."

Just then, Parsley strolled through the lobby like he owned the joint.

Kay shook her head. "That cat. The moment your mom and dad set foot on the property, he came out of nowhere and attached himself to them. He's been following them around like a shadow."

Sage crouched and rubbed his head, right above his ears. "I wish you'd tell us where they got to."

He blinked up at her. For one surreal moment, I almost thought he was going to answer her. Then he yawned widely and started to bathe his front paws with his tongue.

Sage stood. Before we walked out of the lobby, I caught her arm.

"If we can't go to the police, then we have to tell the guys. Mom and Dad told Kay Rosemary was abducted. That changes things. She's definitely not off somewhere working through her nerves like a runaway bride. She needs our help," I said. I jutted out my chin, prepared to argue the point.

But there was no need.

She nodded. "You're right. Let's go."

As soon as we turned the corner near the parlor where the men were putting together the gift bags we heard raucous laughter floating down the hallway.

When we walked into the room, Dave stood up and waved his hand with a flourish to show off their work.

I nodded approvingly at the tidy rows of favors. Despite—or maybe because of—the collection of empty beer bottles, they'd completed the project in almost no time.

Victor grinned at me. "We finished your job, so it's time to celebrate."

I managed a wan smile.

"Right, let's get Rosemary. I propose a game of bocce out on the lawn," Dave said.

"Boys versus girls," Roman added.

Sage let out a long, shaky breath. "Rosemary's missing."

The air in the room seemed to still, and the men fell silent. Dave placed his hands palms down on the table and leaned forward. Roman scrunched his forehead into a squiggle of concern. And Victor watched me with wide, worried eyes.

"Rosemary's missing?" Dave echoed in a soft, controlled voice that belied the tightness of his face. "What do you mean, missing?"

"After Chelle made the last-minute alterations to the wedding dress, Rosemary tried it on, just like we told you. I left to get Sage so she could see, too. When we got back to her room, Rosemary was gone, and the French doors leading from her room out to the patio were open." I said.

I glanced down and realized my hands were shaking as I spoke. Victor must have noticed, too, because he took my hand in his and gave it a reas- suring squeeze.

"You don't think she got cold feet, do you?" Victor whispered, his mouth near my ear.

Dave's eyes narrowed as if he'd heard.

"No," I said simply, locking eyes with Dave. "Rosemary didn't vanish because she was unsure about getting married. I'm sure of it."

Dave bobbed his head in acknowledgment, but I knew his next question would be to ask why we hadn't told him Rosemary was missing when we ran into him outside her room. Sage knew it, too.

She headed him off. "We didn't tell you when we saw you before because there was one more place we needed to look first. We didn't want to worry you for no reason."

"But you've checked that place and didn't find her?" Roman prompted her gently.

"Right."

I had no idea whether that response was going to satisfy her boyfriend or a homicide detective, but Victor's reporter instincts were never going to let it stand unchallenged.

Sure enough, he tilted his head and asked "Where did you check?"

But before Sage could answer, Dave had pulled out his cell phone.

"What are you doing?" I asked him.

"Calling the local police, of course. Unless you've already done that?"

Sage crossed the room and put her hand on his arm. "Please don't."

"Why?" he demanded, his finger still hovering over the numbers.

"Please, put your phone away and I'll explain."

Rosemary's fiancé gave Sage a long, warning

look but pocketed his phone. "Start talking," he said.

"Thank you. To answer Victor's question, the other place we looked for her was in one of the cottages. Did you notice the bird watchers roaming around the resort?"

"The older couple in full safari gear? Yeah, they're sort of hard to miss," he countered.

She gave a wry smile. "Yeah. Not one of my better plans, admittedly. They were supposed to blend. They're not birding enthusiasts. They're our parents. And they're staying in the Rose Cottage."

"Your parents are here?" Dave asked in disbelief.

Roman and Victor wore bewildered expressions. I knew the feeling.

Sage explained, the words coming out fast, tripping over one another. "I guess our mother and Aunt Ruby must stay in touch somehow. After Rosemary sent out the wedding invitations, Aunt Ruby must've told Mom. And, long story short, Mom called me and asked me to help her figure out a way for her and my dad to be here for the wedding."

A thundercloud crossed Dave's face. "Did Rosemary find out about this? Because, if she did, I guarantee that's why she took off." His voice broke with emotion—anger and worry.

Roman put a hand on Dave's shoulder. "It's going to be okay, man. We'll find her."

"He's right. If the five of us work together, we *will* find her," I said. "And before you ask, no, I didn't know anything about this harebrained scheme to bring my parents to the resort. That was all Sage ... and a couple of Mom and Dad's friends."

Sage's cheeks turned deep pink and she dropped her eyes to the floor. My heart gave a tug, and I instantly felt guilty.

I went on, "I understand why Sage did it, though. And I think, in her heart, Rosemary will understand, too. But that's sort of irrelevant now, because Rosemary is missing. And so are our parents."

Sage gave me a tremulous smile of thanks. Then Roman walked around the table to put his arm around her waist in a show of support.

"Your parents are missing, too?" Roman asked.

"We think they went after Rosemary. That's why we can't call the police," Sage explained. "Given the circumstances, there are probably more than a few law enforcement agencies who would be interested to learn they're back in the United States. So can we please try to find them ourselves first?"

Her eyes swept the room but landed on Dave and stayed there. Dave worked his jaw, thinking.

Victor cleared his throat. "Thyme and I have a little experience with this issue, you know. When my sister went missing I refused to involve the police because I wasn't sure whether her ex-husband had a friend on the force. So, while I imagine it must go against everything you believe, Dave, I can see where Sage and Thyme are coming from."

Everyone looked at Dave, waiting to hear what he would say.

The muscle in his left cheek twitched. Then he said in a thick voice, "I don't like it. But I under-stand. That said, if we haven't found her by night-fall, I'm going to the police, and it won't be up for discussion."

"That's fair—more than fair," Sage agreed quickly.

"Thank you," I added.

"So, where do we start?" Roman asked, clap-ping his hands together. He moved toward the door.

"Wait. There's a few more details we need to tell you," I said. "There was a man hanging around outside the seamstress's shop in town today. He was watching me."

Victor purred. "That's because you're hot."

I rolled my eyes and swatted at him. "I'm being serious. I think he might've followed me back to the resort."

"And Rosemary said she saw a stranger wandering around down on the beach during the rehearsal before that," Sage added.

Dave frowned. Victor frowned. Roman frowned. I'm sure I was frowning, too.

"Then, when the cottage was empty, we asked Kay if she had any idea where our parents were. She said they'd come running into the lobby, yammering about an abduction. They borrowed the pickup truck and took off."

"We think they must have been skulking around and saw Rosemary being taken. So, if we find them, we'll find her. Or the other way around," Sage said, finishing our story breathlessly.

Dave turned ashen, but when he spoke, he used his dispassionate detective voice. "Here's how we're going to do this. Thyme and Victor, go back to town. Talk to Chelle. Find out what, if anything, your parents might have told her about Rosemary's disappearance. And keep an eye out to see if this stranger pops up again. I'm going to go to Rosemary's room and poke around. Sage and Roman, go back to the cottage and check inside—see if the Fields left anything behind that would hint at where they could be."

We all bobbed our heads in understanding.

"And make sure your cell phones are fully charged," Victor ordered.

That particular instruction was probably meant for me. I was the queen of the dead mobile phone.

"One last thing," Dave said grimly, sweeping his eyes around the room before he continued. "I know you've all played amateur sleuth in the past. We're not doing that this time. We are going to safely and maturely search for Rosemary."

He pointed at Sage, "In other words, don't crash any golf carts through any windows."

Sage nodded, her lips pressed together in a thin line. I giggled, which was a bad move.

He turned in my direction. "And you. There won't be a gun-toting Mother Superior to save your bacon this time if you decide to take on a psychopath single-handedly."

The laughter died in my throat. "Got it."

"Good. Now let's go. We need to find my bride." Dave strode through the open door without looking back to confirm we were following behind. We were.

CHAPTER 16

ROSEMARY

"Say, Rosie, do you know why chicken coops only have two doors?"

I kept my eyes firmly closed and sat motionless against the wall of the storage container and waited. I knew my father well enough to know my silence wasn't going to be a deterrent to his punch line.

He gave it a moment just in case I was going to respond. When it became clear to him that I wasn't, he said, "Because if they had four doors, they'd be chicken sedans." He cackled softly.

I kept my face impassive, careful not to move a muscle, emit a groan, or otherwise indicate that I'd heard him. He lapsed into blessed silence for almost thirty seconds, then said, "If seagulls fly over the sea, what kind of gulls fly over the bay?"

"Oh, Bart, just leave her be. Rosemary never was easy to cajole. You're not going to jolly her into talking to us with your lame jokes," my mother scolded him.

"Rosemary can't resist a good chuckle. The answer is a bagel, by the way. Bay gull, bagel; get it?"

I was feeling more like a French existentialist by the moment. Without opening my eyes, I said, "I'm not responding to your jokes because I'm sleeping."

"You're not asleep," he protested.

I opened my right eye. "Let's pretend I am anyway." I closed it in a hurry to block out the sight of sadness crossing his face at my cold tone.

I regretted snapping at my dad pretty much instantly because my mom decided to fill the silence by peppering me with stored-up questions about my personal life. "We *are* all stuck here together, Rosemary. Why not be nice and tell us about your David. Where did you meet? How did you know he was the one? What does he do?"

I opened both eyes this time and ignored her

questions to pose one of my own. "How do you know his name is David?" Before she could answer, I hit her with my follow-up question. "And how did you just happen to turn up at the resort this weekend?"

My parents exchanged a look. I already had a pretty good idea as to who might've told them, but I wanted to see if Mom and Dad would be honest with me.

My mother plucked at the hem of her khaki jacket absently while she formed her answer. "Well, honey, I stay in contact with your Aunt Ruby. Not that often, but every now and again. And I just happened to get a new burner phone a day or two after she received your invitation in the mail. So, of course, she mentioned it."

Of course. I left aside the incongruity of my mother tossing around the phrase 'burner phone' as if it were 'lemon balm' or 'skein of yarn' and focused on the incompleteness of her answer. "That may have happened. But there's no way Aunt Ruby helped you come up with this ridiculous ornithology cover story and snuck you into the resort and into one of the cottages."

"True, true," my father agreed.

"And Simon as your alias? That has Kay written all over it."

Dad laughed. "Yes, Kay helped."

"Anybody else?"

"Chelle," my mom admitted in a small voice.

Chelle, who had created the beautiful gown I was currently dragging through dust and dirt, had been keeping a giant secret from me. I looked down at the cream-colored skirt involuntarily.

"It's gorgeous. And you're lovely in it—even more so than the picture she texted me," Mom said.

"You're the out-of-town friends she's visiting with tomorrow, aren't you? That's why she's not coming to the wedding." Pieces of the puzzle were starting to fit together.

My dad smiled sadly. "You always have been a smart cookie, honey. Yes, Chelle didn't want us to be alone. She planned to sit with us under that stand of elm trees and watch from a distance."

I ignored the wave of sympathy and tenderness welling up inside me and pushed on. "But, let's be honest. Ruby, Kay, Chelle—none of them was the mastermind behind this harebrained scheme. Was it Sage or was it Thyme?" I demanded.

My parents exchanged another look. Then my father mimed zipping his mouth shut, while my mom turned an invisible key over her lips and tossed it into the corner.

"Very mature."

We lapsed back into silence, and I thought it through. Thyme was a realist. Sage was the one who harbored fantasies of a familial reconciliation worthy of a movie on the Hallmark Channel.

"Sage," I muttered, more to myself than to them.

My dad's blue eyes sagged with worry. "Don't be mad at her, Rosie Posie. She just wants—"

"I know what she wants. She wants us to pretend to be one big happy family, She wants me to forget you abandoned us, saddling us with *your* debt, so you could shirk your responsibilities and sail off, literally, into the sunset."

"Rosemary, please, don't ever say we abandoned you. That's not the choice we made. We panicked. We knew we were in over our heads, and we couldn't imagine being strong enough to make things right. But we knew you girls were." My mother's tone had started off sharp, almost as biting as my own; but, by the end, her voice was breaking.

She sagged against my father's shoulder, and he wrapped his arms round her. "Don't cry, love." He patted her back and then turned to face me.

"We're going to make things right. That's why we intercepted the ransom demand and followed you here. We're going to get you out of this."

I stared, hoping I'd misheard. "There was a ransom demand? And you ... *took* it? So, not only does nobody know where I am, they don't know what these guys want?" I was shaking with anger. "You asked about my fiancé? He's *a police detective*. He's far better equipped to handle a kidnapping than two aging hippies are."

My mother's eyes flashed. "Rosemary Harmony Love Field, I'll remind you we are still your parents, not just two random aging hippies. And your father and I are trying to fix this mess." She yanked a folded piece of paper out of one of the multitude of pockets in her khaki vest. "This ransom demand came from Hercules. This is still about us."

She shook the paper at me crazily. I snatched it out of her hand and scanned it. He wanted one hundred thousand dollars to be delivered to the old bank in town by six p.m.

I shook my head in confusion. "Herk the Jerk. I don't understand. We don't owe him anything anymore. The remaining debt is all held by a legitimate bank. Hercules isn't even in the picture."

"Payback," my father said.

I sighed. In what should come as no surprise to anyone, my sisters and I didn't have an extra hundred grand lying around.

"Where are we, anyway?" I asked, realizing they would know, since they presumably hadn't traveled here in the cargo hold of a windowless panel van.

"Halfway between Seashore and Atlantic City," my dad told me. "I imagine Hercules is at least a part owner of this storage facility. And I'm sure any partners he may have are from the Atlantic City area."

Even without his meaningful tone, I would've caught his drift. "Mob."

"Probably," my mother agreed. Then her curiosity got the better of her, and she switched gears. "So, you're going to marry a police detective. Not who I would've imagined for you. How did you meet?"

"Not now, please, Mom. We need to focus on getting ourselves out of here. Do either of you have any brilliant ideas?"

They stared at me blankly for a moment. Then my father shook his head. "No. We were hoping we could find Hercules and reason with him."

I held my tongue as to my thoughts about that plan and moved on. "Okay, I have nothing with me. No shoes, no phone, nothing. I assume Mr. Hospitality out there took your cell phones and car keys?"

They nodded.

"What about your Swiss Army knife?"

My father always had a Swiss Army knife attached to his belt loop. He looked down at the spot where it should have been. "He took that, too."

I appraised my parents. "Well, between the two of you, you have about a million pockets. What *didn't* he take?"

My dad started patting himself down. "I have my antacids." He reached into his breast pocket and removed a small pouch. "Would either of you like one?" he asked proffering the package as if it contained after-dinner mints and not chalky sodium bicarbonate.

We both shook our heads.

"No thanks, Dad. But maybe you want to dissolve one. Is your indigestion bothering you?"

"I'm fine, pumpkin. Just fine." He finished searching his pockets. "Well, that's about it."

"Bart, what about your cash?" Mom asked anxiously. "Did that man take it from you?"

"No, love, not to worry. I left it in the room."

"But how are we going to pay the ransom without it?" she persisted.

I didn't want to know any details if my father had a hundred thousand dollars socked away in his underwear drawer. I turned to my mother and asked, "What about you, Mom? Do you have a nail file, cuticle scissors—anything we could conceivably use as a weapon?"

My mother's eyes widened in shock at the notion of attacking our captor, but she shook her head no. "Let's see. I have a small bottle of essential oils. Frankincense, I think. And some chewing gum."

Unlike Dad, she didn't offer me a piece of gum.

I exhaled, thinking. I reached for one of the bottles of now-very warm water and took a swig. "How do we get ourselves out of here with the package of fizzy tablets, a bottle of essential oils, and a pack of gum?"

It didn't look promising.

Ever the completist, my mother added, "And some half-empty bottles of water."

I almost rolled my eyes, but the memory of an experiment I'd done with Dylan and Skylar, the kids in the family Sage works for, stopped me cold. My irritation turned to excitement, and I laughed.

"What's so funny, honey?" Mom asked.

"I have an idea." It wasn't elegant, but it might be serviceable.

CHAPTER 17

SAGE

*A*s soon as Roman and I got outside and headed back along the path I had just walked with my sister, he took my hand in his. I waited for him to ask why I hadn't told him about my parents, but he didn't.

"I'm sorry I didn't tell you," I said after a moment's silence.

He shook his head. "No. You don't owe me an apology or an explanation."

I managed a smile.

Then he went on, "But I have to tell you ... I thought we already learned our lesson about secrets."

His voice was measured, showing no sign of disappointment or anger. But I squirmed under the weight of what he said. He was right, and I knew he was right. His mom's attempt to keep family secrets had unraveled with a lot of fallout. Ever since, he'd tried to practice radical honesty. Muffy, who was his stepmother and my boss, shared Roman's devotion to the truth, the whole truth, and nothing but the truth.

And while I understood intellectually that secrets inevitably came to light, emotionally, I just hadn't been able to bring myself to be open with him about my parents.

"I know. I did want to tell you, but I knew if I told you I'd have to tell Rosemary and Thyme, too. And that would've been ugly."

"You mean because Rosemary wouldn't want them at her wedding? Don't you think that was her decision to make, Sage?"

I nodded miserably. The truth was, though, I thought I knew better than she did. I had convinced myself that Rosemary was holding on to anger toward our parents and that her grudge was unhealthy and unproductive. But, to be totally honest, I was holding on to an improbable fantasy of being a functional family.

We reached the front door of the cottage.

"Do you have the master key?" he asked.

"I don't need it. Unless things have changed dramatically, my mother wouldn't have locked the door behind her." I turned the handle and, sure enough, the door swung open.

Roman gawked in amazement. There was no way to explain Mary Jane Field's belief that barriers to community, such as locked doors, served only to create negative energy without sounding like I was on a mystical trip of my own, so I just walked inside. After a few seconds, he followed and turned on the light by the door.

The cottage was tidy. Aside from the field guides and birding manuals stacked on the small table there was little physical evidence to show the cottage was occupied. The unmistakable scent of patchouli hanging on the air left no doubt someone with an affinity for incense was in residence. Roman wrinkled his nose, and I laughed. For me, the smell was redolent of my childhood and brought happy memories rushing back.

"What exactly are we supposed to be looking for, do you think?" I asked.

Roman considered the question then shrugged. "I guess something tied to Rosemary's disappearance. I don't know. Remember, you're the Field sister dating the golf caddy, not the one dating the homicide detective."

I leaned over and kissed his cheek. "Right. I'm the one dating the caddy who helped solve a murder and put a blackmailer in jail," I reminded him.

I moved through the seating area and poked around the kitchenette but didn't find anything of interest. Roman crouched and opened a small refrigerator set under the counter.

"Almond milk, rice milk, soy milk, and hemp milk. What's wrong with milk milk?" he asked as he twisted his neck to peer up at me.

I shook my head. "Dad likes options. But not the exploitation of our friends in the bovine world."

I wondered if Roman would get the chance to meet my parents. I'd met his mom and his passel of aunts and I worked for and lived with his dad, step-mom, half-brother, and half-sister. I tried to picture Roman meeting Bart and Mary Jane, but my imagination failed me. He closed the refrigerator and joined me in the hallway outside the bedroom.

I really didn't relish the idea of snooping through my parents' bedroom. But if there was a chance it could help us find my sister, I'd do it. I opened the deep drawer in the bedside table. My mother's embroidered pouch-style bag was folded neatly inside. I removed it from the drawer, eased the zipper open, and peered into it; it held a bottle of citronella and geranium oil, which she had used as a bug repellant for as long as I could remember; a dog-eared paperback copy of *A Room of One's Own*; two passports rubber-banded together; and a handful of chamomile tea sachets.

"Nothing helpful," I announced with relief.

"Sage."

I turned at the clear alarm ringing in Roman's voice. He had opened the top dresser drawer and was holding a thick wad of cash. My father's familiar silver money clip hardly seemed up to the task of containing the bills.

"These are all hundreds." He waved the clip at me.

"I'm sure they pay cash for everything. They can't risk leaving any sort of paper or electronic trail, you know?" I had long since internalized the reality that my parents were on the lam. But I could see the realization hitting Roman that his girlfriend was the daughter of a pair of criminals. Not just criminals, international criminals.

He held my gaze for a long moment then slid the money back into the drawer.

"Let's go. We're not going to find anything here."

We ran into Dave just outside the cottage door.

"Hey," I said, pulling the door closed behind me.

"Aren't you going to lock that?" Dave wanted to know.

Roman snorted. "Don't ask. Did you find anything interesting in Rosemary's room?"

Dave leaned forward and spoke with an intensity completely at odds with his usual genial temperament. The last time I'd seen him so serious was when I met him in Los Angeles, and he was investigating Rosemary as a murder suspect.

"I did," he said now, energy thrumming in his voice. "There were four sets of footprints in the garden outside the patio."

"Four?" I echoed.

I hadn't even thought to look for footprints. Maybe that's why I was an accountant turned nanny, and not a detective.

"And a fifth set further back near the blueberry bushes," he continued.

"Five sets of footprints?" Roman mused. "Some of those must have been us, though. Right?"

I nodded. It had to be.

"Nope," Dave said with certainty, ticking off on his fingers as he spoke. "One set belongs to Rosemary. She was barefoot when Thyme left her, and her bare toes left an impression in the mulch."

"Her sandals are still in her room," I confirmed.

He twisted his mouth into a frown. "She was dragged off the patio through the garden, judging by the tracks. Her abductor is a big, heavy person—likely male—going by the depth and size of his shoe prints. And, at some point, her prints disappear and his get deeper."

"As if he picked her up and carried her," Roman mused.

"Right. The extra weight would have caused a deeper impression. Now, Rosemary's wiry, but she's strong from all that catering. So, this guy has to be fairly competent to have managed to carry her off. We're looking for a big, strong man."

"She would have fought him like a hellcat," I murmured.

Dave flashed a hint of a smile my way. "Yes, she would have."

After a brief silence, Roman cleared his throat. "What about the other three sets of footprints?"

"Two of them belong to Mr. and Mrs. Field. I'm almost certain of it. They seem to have been crouched in some hedges that afforded a good view of Rosemary's room. They must've have stayed there for a while, watching her. They would have been concealed from both Rosemary and her kidnapper by an overhang of blooming branches. Oh, also, the little enclosure smells like patchouli."

"That was them," Roman agreed with a glance back at the cottage. "The breeze died down this afternoon, I guess the scent is still hanging on the air."

"So my parents would have seen Rosemary being abducted, which squares with what Kay said."

"Right," Dave said, his expression still tight.

"And the final set of prints?" I asked.

He furrowed his brow. "Someone wearing men's dress shoes was standing in the copse of blueberry bushes just up the hill from the garden. He definitely would have been able to see the abduction from where he was."

"Men's dress shoes," I mused.

"Thyme's suit guy," Roman said.

Dave's eyes sparked with interest. "A witness. Call Thyme and see if she's seen any trace of him in town."

CHAPTER 18

I parked the car Victor had rented for the weekend into a spot two doors down from the Sugar Plum.

"There's an open spot right in front of the dress shop," Victor said as he got out of the car.

"I know. I thought we could walk a bit and see if anyone's following us before we go strolling into Chelle's place. You know?" Even though she hadn't hesitated to meddle in our family business, I definitely didn't want to bring trouble to Chelle's door.

"Good point."

We sauntered up Main Street, taking our time stopping and looking in shop windows. The sidewalks were mostly empty, and I didn't have the feeling we were being followed or watched.

"Are any alarm bells ringing for you?" I asked.

Victor scanned both sides of the street casually. "No," he said. "I think your guy's gone."

We passed the candy shop and stopped in front of Chelle's Sea Belles. I rang the bell. After several seconds had passed, I cupped my hands together and peered through the window where I'd been sitting just hours earlier.

"Her sign says the shop's closed," Victor pointed out.

"I know. But she usually closes around four and spends a couple hours catching up on paperwork and working on her sketches and patterns. Maybe she stepped out to get something to eat."

"Well that's just great. We don't really have time for wasted trips if we're going to find your sister before nightfall."

"I guess I should have called first." I dug my phone out of my bag and selected Chelle's number.

After three rings, she answered.

"This is Chelle."

"Hi, it's Thyme."

"Is something wrong with the dress?" she asked worriedly.

"No, I'm not calling about the dress." I knew the best way to approach the subject would be to ease into it, but Victor was right; we were running out of time. So I plunged right in. "Rosemary's missing. We think she may have been abducted from the resort ... and my parents might know something about it."

"Oh, Thyme—"

"I don't care that you were in on the secret. I just need to know whether you talked to them after Rosemary disappeared," I assured her. It was mostly true.

She exhaled. "Your mom called about an hour after you left with the dress. She said some goon had grabbed Rosemary outside her room, and she and your dad were going after her. She had it in her head that it was related to their financial troubles, but she didn't tell me why she made that connection."

"Did she tell you where they were going?"

"I'm sorry, honey, but she didn't. She was really upset. We didn't talk long. I tried to convince her to call the police, but she wouldn't hear of it. She kept saying she'd caused this mess, and she'd fix it."

My heart fluttered. It was what we'd suspected, but knowing for sure my parents had gone off to save Rosemary ramped up my already considerable anxiety. Victor took my hand in his. I gripped his tightly.

"Okay. She hasn't called you back, has she?"

"No," Chelle said mournfully. "And I've tried her phone several times. Either her battery is dead or it's turned off. My calls are going straight to voicemail."

"Will you let me know if you hear from her?"

"I will," she promised.

"Ask her about the guy in the suit." Victor stage whispered beside me.

"I have one more question. There was a man out on the street when I left with the dress—"

"The gentleman in the suit?" she broke in.

"Yes!"

"He was standing across the street in front of the bank. I only noticed him because he noticed you. He watched you get in the truck and then ran, literally ran, to his car and tore off after you. I almost called to warn you in case he was planning to follow you, but he caught the light at the corner. And you know that light —it's gotta be the longest traffic light in the county. You were probably home by the time it turned green."

I managed a weak laugh. "Did you recognize him?"

"Never saw him before in my life. And what kind of wacko wears a suit in Seashore?"

"Okay, well, I have to go. But don't forget to call me if you talk to my parents."

"Don't worry, I will. Oh, I jotted down his license plate. Do you want it?"

My eyes bugged out. "The man in the suit's?"

"Sure. He was at the red light long enough for me to get a pen and paper."

Victor must have heard enough to follow the conversation because he was grinning like a kid.

"Yes, please."

She rattled off the plate, I repeated it, and Victor scribbled it in his reporter's notebook.

"That's it. It was a District of Columbia plate," she added.

I thanked her and ended the call.

"Lucky break she got his plate," Victor said.

"No kidding. Let's call and tell the others."

"I want to check one more thing first."

"What?" I was impatient to call back to the resort with a promising lead. And I sort of figured we'd earned a treat. The Sugar Plum was just steps away, after all. It would be a shame to a waste a trip into town.

Victor stepped up to the curb. "I want to go to the bank across the street where he was standing."

"Why?" We weren't going to find cupcakes outside the abandoned bank building. At least, not any cupcakes I'd want to consume.

"Old reporter's trick. It always helps to see a scene from the subject's vantage point."

We crossed the street, and I tried to keep my grumbling to the bare minimum. We stopped in front of the bank building and looked in the window. All I saw was a dusty, empty lobby. I turned to snark at Victor, but he wasn't looking inside. He had turned and was staring toward Chelle's boutique.

"Where were you parked?" he asked.

"Right in front of the dress shop."

My cell phone's ringtone began to play "The 59th Street Bridge Song," more commonly known as "Feelin' Groovy."

"It's Sage," I said as I reached into my bag for the phone. Rosemary's was "Homeward Bound." The ringtones were a nod to the album that had given us our names.

Victor leaned casually against the building's façade looking out over the square.

"I was just about to call you. Mom and Dad did

see Rosemary's kidnapping. They told Chelle they were going to go after her," I said as soon as I picked up the call.

"That sounds right. Dave found five sets of footprints in the gardens on the grounds outside of Rosemary's room. They belong to Rosemary; the guy who grabbed her; mom and dad; and, we think, the stranger in the suit. Mom and dad and the suit guy all would have had a view of her being abducted."

"That man in the suit is like a bad penny," I muttered. "But, listen, Chelle got his license plate number."

"That's great. Give it me and I'll see if Dave can have a friend run it."

I read off the D.C. plate number from Victor's notebook and she read it back to me.

"That's it," I said absently, staring into the darkened bank's interior. A thought was nibbling at my brain—the way I should be nibbling at a dark chocolate-covered cake pop from the Sugar Plum.

"What is it?" Sage asked.

"What is what?"

"You sound a million miles away."

"I'm getting an idea," I said, as my train of thought began to take shape.

I felt Victor's attention slide from the street over to me, his curiosity no doubt piqued by the excitement in my voice.

"You need to pull together a list of properties that had mortgages with the bank when it closed," I told my older sister.

"Excuse you?" she bristled.

"Herk's the most likely person to be behind Rosemary's disappearance. And if this is some sort of demented ploy to pay us back for cutting him out of the loans, then he probably has her stashed in one of the other properties impacted by the bank's closure."

"Why do you say that?" she demanded.

"Because Herk didn't just take over Mom and Dad's loan. He went around buying up the debt from all the local businesses that couldn't meet the New York bank's more rigorous lending requirements. And, realistically, that was probably most of them. He'd have put the squeeze on everybody, not just the resort. So, by now, there's a good chance he owns a property where he could hide a kidnapping victim. Maybe a rental beach house or something, I don't know. That's why we need the list," I explained as the pieces started to fall into place.

Beside me, Victor nodded his agreement.

"Maybe," Sage said. "But why do you want me to do this—couldn't you ask around town?"

I snorted. "That's not exactly efficient. Besides, you were a forensic accountant. There must be online databases you can access that show ownership information, loan details, and other gobbledygook. Aren't there?"

"Sure, but I can't just pull together a list by snapping my fingers. It's going to take time."

Out of the corner of my eye, I noticed Victor waving and pointing his thumb at his chest. "If you want, Victor can help with it. He's a business reporter, after all. He probably speaks your language."

"Okay," Sage said, warming to the idea.

Victor was staring at the bank window. "Thyme," he said.

I shot him a look that said 'dude, I'm on the phone.'

"Thyme," he repeated urgently, tapping on the glass.

"Hang on a sec," I told my sister.

I scooted over to the other end of the window to see what had caught his attention. It was a yellowing flyer from the summer the bank closed. The sheet announced the sale of several commercial properties at auction. Given the timing and the locations, they almost had to have been bank customers. I'll Dye for You (the hair salon that had predated Clare's), an auto body repair shop that also serviced farm equipment, and a storage facility out on the road that led to the Garden State Parkway.

I looked at Victor. "You think it's one of these?"

"Either the storage facility or the mechanic shop. I'd bet anything."

I recognized the thrill of the chase in his words. He was using his reporter-on-a-story voice.

"Hey, Sage, Victor has an idea." I'm putting him on." I passed the phone to Victor.

"Hi. Listen, I don't think we need to do the research Thyme just asked for, after all. I think she's on the right track, but we can narrow the field down to two properties. I'm looking at a flyer posted in the front window of that old bank. There's an auto body shop on Ocean Road. And a storage facility ... right, Uncle Jed's, that's it."

He was bouncing on the balls of his feet, full of energy, like a puppy in need of a long walk and a ball to chase. "If you could just pull commercial transfer records and find out if that loan shark has an interest in either of those properties, I think that's our starting point."

He and Sage went back and forth a few times, trading phrases like real estate investment trust, and limited liability partner. I surveyed the street, listening with one ear to Victor speaking financialese.

I found myself wondering whether the Sugar Plum still made those white chocolate and apricot scones dusted with crystallized ginger. They were great with a cup of tea. Or I could go for a couple caramel brownie bites. I checked my watch, wondering what time the sweets shop closed out of season.

I was just about to cross the street to see if it was my lucky day, when Victor dashed my sugary dreams by exclaiming, "We'll meet you there. Leaving now."

He ended the call and handed me back my phone.

"Where are we going now?"

"Herk has an interest in the REIT that owns Uncle Jed's Storage Yard."

"What's a REIT?"

"It stands for Real Estate Investment Trust."

I grumped my way back to the car. I'd been this close to a delicious infusion of sugar and fat.

"How do we even know it's the storage place and not the auto body shop?" I demanded as I flung myself into the passenger seat and tossed him the keys.

"You want me to drive?"

"Yeah, my blood sugar's too low. I'm starving," I muttered darkly.

He turned and looked at me before he started the engine. "You know, Thyme, we've been dating for a while now."

I folded my arms across my chest and eyed him cautiously. "So?"

"So, this isn't my first time at the rodeo. I know the hour or so before dinner is your witching hour. Open the glove compartment."

I gave him another suspicious look, but did as he as he instructed. A bonanza of snack bars, dried fruit, and chocolates cascaded out into my lap. Like manna from heaven.

My mood instantly lightened, and I turned to beam at my beloved. "Thanks," I said unwrapping a truffle.

"No need to thank me. It's really a matter of self-preservation. To answer your question. The auto body shop burned down two years ago." He started the car and pulled out onto the road.

"Did Herk own that, too?"

"Yes. It was owned by the same REIT. I'm guessing they committed arson in furtherance of insurance fraud and then let the property sit empty. It hasn't been resold and no building permits have been issued."

"Okay, the storage yard it is," I mumbled around a mouthful of chocolate goodness.

CHAPTER 19

ROSEMARY

"*N*ow, where did you learn about this explosion? Was it part of your course work?" my dad asked.

I had instantly regretted using the word 'explode.' Both of my parents were looking at me with so much hope in their eyes that I just knew I was going to let them down in a big way.

"It won't really be an explosion," I explained for what felt like the seventeenth time, careful to keep my tone patient. "There will be a chemical reaction between the bicarbonate of soda in the antacid and the hot water. It's not dissimilar to the fizzing that happens when you drop one of the tablets in a glass of water to drink it, Dad. But, here we're going to add four or maybe even six of the tablets broken in half to a bottle of pretty warm water and put the cap back on really tight. The water and the tablets will react to create CO_2—carbon dioxide gas—which is going to build up so much pressure that it'll launch the cap right off and make a pretty big bang.

My mom giggled with excitement.

I frowned. "It's going to be more like a fire-cracker than anything. But if we time things just right, the next time that big lump of sparkling personality comes to check on us, it should be enough of a distraction that we can rush the door and surprise him. Then we just need to hope we're faster than he is. But you shouldn't expect a big cloud of smoke or anything."

"What if we put in the whole package of tablets?" my dad asked eagerly.

"I think the most we can hope for is a loud noise. A half-dozen tablets will be more than enough," I cautioned.

The water bottle rocket was a time-honored elementary school science experiment. It wasn't going to take my sophisticated knowledge of chemistry to pull it off. What it *was* going to take was impeccable timing. And a dollop of luck.

My mom seemed to know what I was thinking.

"Don't worry, Rosie, the Universe is on our side."

"Oh, but we'll have to get the keys to the truck from him," I suddenly realized, feeling sick to my stomach. No chance.

"Turn that frown upside down, sweetheart," my dad ordered. "Your mother can hot wire that old pickup in ten seconds flat."

I stared at my parents. My father was visibly proud of his wife's questionable talent. My mom was blushing and grinning.

"Is that really true?"

"Sure. I kept losing the keys that year I was so busy with my campaign."

Ah, her ill-fated run for the school board.

"Okay?" I prompted.

"And I couldn't waste time searching for them. I had events to attend. So, I watched some videos on the Internet and taught myself how to turn over the engine without the keys."

"What if it's locked?"

"Oh, I never lock it," she assured me.

"Well, Igor or whatever his name is might have."

My father straightened his shoulders. "I'll break the glass if it's locked. Stop worrying. Devoting energy to things you don't want to happen just brings them into existence. You should know that."

I held my tongue rather than get sucked into a discussion about his favorite topic of manifesting one's own destiny.

We sat for several moments in tense and silent anticipation of hearing footsteps and gravel. But as the minutes stretched on and no one approached the storage pod, my adrenaline waned. I felt myself slumping back into a cloud of despair.

My mother must've noticed the change in my demeanor because she suddenly struck up a conversation to distract me from my misery. "We saw you gathering lavender earlier. Is that for the flower arrangements?"

"No, I'm making Grandma Bay's honeysuckle lemon cake with lavender cream," I told her.

"For the wedding?"

I nodded. "Right."

"That's quite an ambitious undertaking." She gave me a worried look.

"I do run my own catering business, Mom. Trust me, I've made plenty of much fancier wedding cakes for much bigger weddings than mine. And, I want to do something personal, something special."

"But you weren't the bride at any of those weddings, were you?" she persisted.

"Point taken."

My father had a different concern. "Why are you running a catering company? What happened to chemistry?"

I wrinkled my forehead in confusion. "Surely, Aunt Ruby told you about Rosemary's Gravy?"

My mom ducked her head and answered in a tiny voice. "She told me. I ... may not have mentioned it to you, Bart."

My father's eyebrows shot up his forehead, so I hurried to answer the question before we had an unplanned explosion in the storage unit.

"I had to leave the lab to make more money after you saddled us with the resort and took off."

A shadow crossed his face, and his energy changed from anger to sorrow.

"But," I continued, "I really love catering. Creating the recipes is part science, part art. And nourishing people brings me a joy I honestly never felt in the research lab. Plus, I'm pretty good at it. I won't rule out going back to chemistry someday, but I really am fulfilled now."

They both smiled. I could see their relief and their pride.

I couldn't believe what I was about to do, but I did it anyway. I squared my shoulders and said, "I guess I owe the fact that I found my calling to the two of you. I never would've had the nerve to start my catering business if I hadn't worked as a private chef first. And I would never have been working as a private chef if I hadn't needed to earn a lot of money fast. So thank you."

I could tell they were both searching my face to see if I was being sarcastic or snarky so I kept my expression perfectly sincere.

"I mean it," I insisted. "And I wouldn't have met Dave, either."

My mom exhaled and crossed the room to wrap her arms around me. "I'm so glad to hear that."

"Me, too," my dad said, blinking rapidly and taking off his glasses to clean them on the hem of his shirt. "How did a caterer and a homicide detective meet?" he mused.

"It's a long story," I deadpanned.

A cold ache that had been lodged in my heart for so long that I no longer felt it started to loosen. I was about to open my mouth and tell my parents I loved them and forgave them when loud footsteps and raised voices sounded outside the door.

We scrabbled to our feet, and my dad tossed me the packet of antacids as the metal door rolled up. No time. I tucked the bag into the bodice of my dress and smoothed the silk. I kicked two of the half-empty water bottles toward the wall behind me and tried not to cry at the fact that we'd missed our chance.

"—going to regret this!" A man was shouting.

The metal scraped to a stop to reveal our captor, gripping his trusty baseball bat with one massive hand and the upper arm of a man wearing a black suit with the other.

The big guy gave the man in the suit a solid push. He stumbled into the pod. Dad caught him and steadied him on his feet.

My mother strode up to the opening. The big guy thwacked the bat in his hand and made a guttural sound of warning. Mom was not impressed.

"Now, you listen here young man, you can't hold us like this. It's inhumane. Tell Herk I demand to see him, right now!"

The guy chortled. "Mr. Hercules will see you when he's ready. Not before the money is delivered. Tick tock."

The mystery of whether the muscle-bound

goon spoke English was solved, but I sort of preferred it when he didn't.

Mom didn't blink. "Food. Fresh water. Access to a bathroom. Or no money. I don't know what Mr. Hercules promised you, but I trust you can do the math to figure out your cut of nothing."

For a moment it looked like he was hard at work on his zero division skills. He scrunched up his face as if he were in pain. Finally, he nodded.

"I will bring peanut butter crackers. More water."

"What about bathrooms?" she insisted

He pointed to an empty water bottle near her feet and gave her an evil smile. She made a disgusted mew, but I could barely contain my glee. The promise of more water and crackers meant he'd be returning—with his hands full. He might even leave his trusty bat behind.

"Lots of crackers, please," I said in my most charming voice, even though I couldn't imagine choking down a cracker at this point.

He eyed me with something like pity. I was sure I did look fairly pitiful. I blinked back at him.

"I will bring crackers and other snacks from the vending machine. As much as I can," he promised.

I smiled. "Thank you. Please hurry."

He nodded, fixed his scowl back in place, and rolled down the door and locked us inside.

My father turned to the newcomer, who hadn't made a sound since being shoved inside the pod, and stuck out his hand. "Hi, I'm Bart Field. Who are you?"

"Colin Morgan, sir. I know who you are." He shook my dad's hand then nodded to Mom. "Mrs. Field." He turned to me. "Ms. Field."

I didn't really have patience for the niceties. "Were you sneaking around the resort today?" I demanded.

"Yes, ma'am. Well, no, ma'am. I was present on the premises doing surveillance."

At the word 'surveillance' my mother's hand floated up to her throat. Dad looked a little gray.

"Surveillance? Who in the hell are you and why are you spying on my wedding?"

He stood up straighter and lifted his chin. "I'm Special Agent Colin Morgan, Criminal Investigation, Internal Revenue Service."

"The IRS has special agents?" I asked.

"Yes, ma'am, we surely do. I'm assigned to the Legal Tax Crimes task force."

"Legal tax crimes?" Suddenly the light began to dawn. "You track down tax evaders, don't you?"

"Affirmative, ma'am." He glanced at my parents, almost apologetically.

I sighed. "Okay, fine. Tell me you have a gun."

Special Agent Morgan coughed into his fist.

"Seriously?" I said.

"Some special agents do carry weapons. But, um, I'm a SA-CIS."

"And I'm a potato, if we're playing a nonsense word game."

"Sorry, ma'am. A SA-CIS is a Special Agent—Computer Investigative Specialist. I have advanced training in computer forensic investigations. That's how I tracked your parents down," he said with a little more gusto than I considered to be polite, given the circumstances. He must have realized his mistake and turned to my parents. "Sorry about that, but you were hard to pin down. I can't believe I finally did it!"

"Good job, Special Agent Morgan," my dad said, giving him a congratulatory slap on the back.

Mom nodded her approval. "We slipped up when we came to the wedding, didn't we?"

"Yes, ma'am."

"I hate to interrupt, but if you don't carry a gun, why were you skulking around in the shadows?"

He turned back to me. "I had a gut feeling your parents would come to your wedding, even though they hadn't been invited." He sniffed with disapproval, then said, "But I couldn't get the task force to sign off on sending a pair of agents. So, here I am."

"There's a task force devoted to me and Bart?" my mom asked.

"Oh, yes, ma'am. You've proved to be very wily," he assured her.

Mom beamed. "Thank you, Special Agent Morgan."

I rolled my eyes. "Please tell me you called for back-up."

He grimaced. "Uh. That's not really how it works."

"I'll take that as a 'no.' Geez, Special Agent Morgan, Dad at least contributed antacids. You're just dead weight."

"Antacids? I don't understand."

"Rosie here's going to make an explosion," my father told him proudly.

I stifled a groan and retrieved the package from the bodice of my gown. "Hand me that water bottle, please, Mom. We need to get in position and be ready this time."

CHAPTER 20

SAGE

Roman, Dave, and I arrived at Uncle Jed's before Thyme and Victor got there. So we circled the gated facility once, slowly, looking for any sign of Rosemary or the pickup truck but saw nothing. Nothing other than the fact that the entire place was fenced and impenetrable by car.

I looked out the window and half-listened as Dave and Roman went back and forth as to the likelihood of successfully crashing the car through the gate.

"It's not possible," Dave said with an air of finality.

"You'd think so. But then again, Sage did

manage to drive a golf cart through a window," Roman countered.

"I don't recommend it," I piped up at the same time that Dave said, "Your girlfriend is a maniac."

All three of us laughed harder than the situation warranted. But we needed to release some tension, and laughing was better than crying. Or putting my head between my knees and hyperventilating.

When the guffaws and giggles faded, I grew serious and said, "Dave, there's something I want to say before Thyme gets here."

He twisted around in the driver's seat to look at me square in the face. "I'm all ears."

Beside him, Roman gave me an encouraging smile.

I took a deep breath. "I was wrong to help my parents sneak into the resort so they could watch your wedding. I'm sorry I did that."

He looked at me for a long moment, then he shook his head. "No, Sage, you weren't wrong. You wanted your mother and father to be here for the wedding. Your instinct was right. It's been bothering me that my parents would be here, but Rosemary's wouldn't. Our marriage is the union of our families, after all." He smiled gently. "But, you may have gone about it all wrong."

I opened my mouth to protest that I hadn't had a choice, but I clamped it shut before the words could escape. It was like Roman and his stepmom loved to say, 'You always have a choice.' I'd had another choice. I just hadn't had the nerve to make it. Besides, nothing undercut an apology like defending the very thing you were apologizing about. I'd come off sounding worse than Dylan and Skylar.

"Thanks for being so understanding," I said smiling back at him. I could tell my smile was wobbly, but it was the best I could manage. At least I wasn't crying.

"Don't thank me yet. There's a good chance Rosemary's going to wring your neck when this whole mess is over."

We all burst out into another round of too-long, too-loud laughter. I had to wonder whether he was right, though. If Rosemary didn't share her fiancé's philosophy, she might just blame me for ruining her wedding.

Although, I supposed I'd have to share the doghouse with Herk the Jerk. Who kidnaps a bride right before her wedding? Well, aside from the

Dread Pirate Roberts in *The Princess Bride*, I mean. But trust me when I say Herk the Jerk is no Westley the Farm Boy/Dread Pirate Roberts.

I glanced out the window and saw Victor pulling into the gas station. "They're here."

"Their car doesn't look any more capable than this one of crashing through that gate," Dave observed.

Roman said, "What we need is a battering ram. I don't suppose anyone has one?"

"No," I told them as Victor parked next to us and Thyme clambered out of the car eating a granola bar, "what we need is an ultra-flexible person who can climb like a monkey. And it just so happens we do have one of those."

We all tumbled out of the Camry and gathered between the two cars so Dave could bring my sister and Victor up to speed.

"The storage facility is secured by a fence around the perimeter. Two gates—one at the front entrance just across the way, the other around back —provide access if you have the code to punch into the little keypad. We obviously don't have Herk's code, so that's not going to be our way in," Dave said. He sounded the way I imagined a football coach would talk to his team before a game. I half expected him to whip out a white board and start drawing Xs, Os, and squiggly lines.

"I suppose one of us could drive right up to the gate and press the intercom button," Victor suggested. "This Herk character has never met me."

"Or me," Dave agreed.

"He hasn't met me either. And it's not completely crazy. We could say we were just driving by and wanted to check out the place to see if it would work to store ... I don't know, our boat or some furniture, whatever," Roman added. "But I think Sage was going to suggest Thyme climb the fence."

Thyme eyed me over her granola bar. "Oh, really?"

"I mean, you could, couldn't you?" I asked.

She gave a little shrug. "Probably."

"You'll have to anyway," Victor told her. "You and Sage won't be able to come in with us. Depending on who comes to the gate, you might be recognized. You two go to the back gate and get over the fence while we provide a distraction."

I had several questions. "One, how am I getting over the gate? I'm not a yogi. Two, assuming we get over, then what? We have no plan. Three, what about Thyme's suit guy? Where is he in all of this? Did a hit on his license plate come back yet?"

"That's way more than three questions," Dave informed me.

"They're multi-part questions."

Thyme shifted her weight from side to side, restless and eager to move. "I'll help you get over."

I threw her a skeptical look.

"You can do it, Sage. I promise."

"Okay," I said reluctantly. "But what about my other questions?"

Dave chewed on his lip for a moment before answering. "To answer your third question, the plates came back registered to the federal government. I don't know which agency yet. Let's assume our friend in the suit is not working with Herk, but also not necessarily an ally."

"He's after our parents," Thyme said.

"Maybe. Maybe not. But if he is, let's hope he shows up soon with the cavalry because to answer Sage's second question, I guess we're winging it."

We looked around the tight circle at one another. A detective, a nanny, a fitness trainer, a reporter, and a caddy. We weren't exactly a commando dream team. Their faces reflected my own worry.

It was Roman who broke the tension. "Hey, come on. All five of us have faced down crazier odds than this. We got this."

Roman's infectious optimism was one of his best qualities. I just hoped it wasn't misplaced.

CHAPTER 21

THYME

I studied the fence. It was six feet tall, made of black metal. The surface was slick and slippery, so not exactly ideal for getting a foothold, and the spear-shaped finials that topped the railhead were, well, pointy. They weren't so wickedly sharp that they'd impale a person or anything, but they definitely wouldn't provide a comfortable landing. I scratched my chin and considered my options.

Sage was standing a foot or so behind me. She leaned forward and whispered, "What do you think?"

What I thought was I should be able vault myself over the fence, but I wasn't so sure about Sage.

What I said was, "Oh, this is going to be a piece of cake. I'm just trying to figure out the best way to do it."

She moved forward to stand closer to me. She looked up at the fence. "I don't know, Thyme ..."

Roman would've given her a pep talk. Dave would've reasoned with her. Victor would have comforted her. And, if Rosemary had been here, she probably would have ordered Sage to get her bony butt up over that fence. But I did none of those.

Sage had only been eighteen months old when I was born. We'd grown up being mistaken for twins by parents at the homeschooling co-op, members of our mother's gardening club, lifeguards at the public beach. Pretty much everyone. Sure, I was close with Rosemary, but I *knew* Sage. I knew what she loved and what she hated. I knew what brought her joy. And I knew her deepest fear—letting down someone she cared about.

So I took both of her hands in mine and stared straight into her eyes. "Listen to me. You're going over that fence with me because I'm afraid to go over it by myself. I don't want to be trapped on the other side alone with the man who kidnapped my sister."

She opened her mouth to respond, but I went on. "It doesn't matter that my boyfriend, your boyfriend, and a police detective are going to come cruising through the front gates. It doesn't matter if mom and dad are there. None of them explored the woods behind the house with me every summer. None of them—not even Rosemary—knows about the year I was afraid to sleep in the dark. I need you there. So we're going to figure out how to get you over that fence, and we're going to do it fast so we can rescue our sister and celebrate her wedding. Okay?"

Sage looked at me for a few seconds then a little smile spread across her face. "Okay."

I smiled back. That settled, I returned my attention to the fence. After a moment, I had my plan worked out.

"I'll go first and balance on top. That way, if you need any help, I'll be able to reach down and give you a hand.

She looked at the fence and then at me. "How exactly are you going to sit on that fence? It has spikes on top!"

"Don't worry about me," I assured her. "You just do what I say."

She nodded her agreement. I slipped off my

sandals and approached the fence in my bare feet. Then I turned, stood with my back nearly touching the metal rails, and squatted, planting my hands on the ground. I ignored the loose gravel cutting into my palms as I lowered myself into crow pose with my knees balanced alongside my elbows.

Once I was sure I had a sturdy base, I scissored my legs straight up then let them rest against the fence. I held the handstand until I felt my toes grip onto the thin metal bars behind me, about four inches below the railhead.

"Holy crow, I hope you don't expect me to do that," Sage muttered. Then she walked over to the gate and started to read out loud the directions posted on a small sign above the keypad, "Press star then your four digit code then pound. Wait for the gate arm to rise completely before driving your vehicle through. Hmm."

I ignored her babbling and tightened my core muscles to prepare to execute a hanging sit up. I knew it was going to be considerably harder to accomplish hanging by my toes than the position I was familiar with: knees over a pull-up bar. But the movement would be the same.

As I crunched up, I stretched my arms forward and grabbed the finials, using them as leverage to hoist myself up the remaining few inches until I was balancing atop the fence.

Meanwhile, Sage was now mumbling to herself and pressing buttons on the keypad. "Okay, first the star button. Let's see? We'll try 4-3-2-1 and then the pound sign." She stepped back and looked expectantly at the gate. Nothing happened.

I was concentrating too hard on keeping my balance to ask her what the devil she thought she was doing. My arms quivered slightly as I slowly stood with my feet planted, straddling finials on both sides.

I was still catching my breath when the pneumatic gate arm shuddered to life. The vibration knocked me off the fence, but I landed in a low crouch on two feet, panting with exertion and surprise.

Sage picked up my sandals and sauntered through the open gate.

"How'd you know the code?" I demanded breathlessly.

"I didn't know the code, but I know human nature from when I used to work in forensic accounting. Most people picked lousy passwords like 1-1-1-1 or 1-2-3-4 to secure really important things like their life savings or their retirement accounts. So, I figured it was a sure bet someone would use something lame like 4-3-2-1 for the password to a storage yard." She grinned at me. "And I was right!"

I gave her a sidelong look. "Well, why did you wait until I was climbing that blasted fence? I could have just walked through, too."

She flashed me a mischievous grin. "What's the matter, Thyme? You're the one who said it would be a piece of cake to vault over the fence. You eat your cake your way, I'll eat mine my way."

I just shook my head at her, determined not to let on that most of my muscles were quaking, and the few that weren't were going to be on fire in a few hours. "Let's focus on finding Rosemary and getting her out of here. If you have any other brilliant insights into human nature in the meantime, feel free to share them, okay?"

"Fair enough."

I wriggled my feet into my sandals and we raced silently through the open space to the shadow of a concrete block building.

"Office?" I whispered.

Sage shook her head. "Storage, I bet. The office would be in the front, don't you think?"

I nodded. We pressed ourselves against the

side of the building and crept forward, headed toward the main entrance, so we could see when the men came in. As we reached the end of the small, square building, I grabbed Sage's arm. Between the building and the first row of storage bays, there was a paved rectangle designated as 'Employee Parking' by a sign stuck in the ground. There were five vehicles parked in the small lot: a white BMW with the vanity plate "H3RQL35" (which was apparently as close to 'Hercules' as he could manage under the byzantine motor vehicle regulations); a nondescript sedan; the resort pickup truck; a white panel van; and a gleaming black Lincoln with D.C. tags.

"Suit guy is here," she breathed.

"And Mom and Dad."

WE DUCKED behind a big metal Dumpster. I pulled out my cell phone and texted Victor to let him know we were inside and how many cars were in the lot. As I was stowing the phone back in my pocket, I heard the crackle of the intercom as an unseen someone in the office answered.

"What do you want?"

'Herk' I mouthed. Sage nodded. We'd both recognize his coarse, gravelly voice anywhere. After all, he'd left us near-daily voicemails full of increasingly rash and enraged threats in the first weeks after our parents skipped out on their debt.

A few seconds later Dave's voice rang out, loud in the still evening air. "My two buddies and I have a fishing boat we need to store come winter. We wanted to see if you have any spots that might work for us."

It seemed to take Herk a long time to respond. I held my breath, waiting for his answer.

Finally, he said, "I'll open the gate. Pull around to the office. I'm getting ready to leave for the night and it's probably too dark see the spots well, but I'll give you some brochures and take a deposit to secure your spot."

"Sounds great," Dave enthused.

After a few seconds, the gate arm swung up, and Dave inched the Camry forward. Sage and I stayed in the shadows and watched our boyfriends and Dave exit the car and head toward the office. My heart was thudding crazily. I had to stop myself from running after them. I spared a glance at Sage. She looked to be fighting the same urge.

Victor stopped just before the threshold and

looked over his shoulder. I couldn't imagine that he could see us in the lengthening shadows, but he seemed to be looking straight at me. He flashed a smile in our direction then followed Roman and Dave into the office.

As soon as they disappeared I turned to Sage and said, "They'll be okay in there, right?"

"Absolutely. I have no doubt the three of them can handle themselves against one scumbag like Herk the Jerk."

She sounded so confident. But I couldn't stop thinking about the other two cars in the lot. Who knew how many people were here or where their loyalties might lie?

Just then the office door banged open and a bald giant of a man, his arms laden with packaged snack foods and bottled waters, stalked through the doorway. I assumed he'd head for one of the cars, but instead he wound his way through the rows of RVs, trailers, and boats squeezed into tight parking spots and headed for the metal structure located at the opposite back corner of the storage yard from where we'd come in.

Sage nudged me. "Why would somebody take a bunch of food and water to a storage shed?"

I stared at her. "I can only think of one reason."

"Me too."

"Let's go."

So we darted across the vast open yard. Our route was more circuitous then the man's because we were zigzagging from vehicle to vehicle, crouching behind trailers and pressing ourselves up against the sides of campers in case he turned around. Luckily, he was moving slowly. Whether his lack of speed was a function of everything he was carrying or his lumbering size, it was easy to keep up with him.

Finally, he stopped in front of the very last unit in the backmost row of attached, metal storage pods. It was the furthest from the office and the main gate. The logical place to stash something or someone you were trying to keep hidden. He balanced the bottled waters and packages of crackers and cookies in the crook of one arm, as he jiggled a key into a large padlock.

I squeezed Sage's arm. "She's in there."

"I know. But what's our move?"

Our move? I had no flipping idea. I could finesse my way over a fence. But that was the full extent of my rescue team abilities. On the edge of panicking, part of me wanted to call Dave and the guys. But the rational part of my brain knew their best contribution right now was keeping Herk occupied and out of our way.

Before I could formulate a plan, the man successfully opened the padlock. As it banged against the metal door, he lost his grip on his armload of provisions. Several bottles of water tumbled to the ground. He cursed loudly in what sounded like a Slavic language then aimed a solid kick at the door.

"He has a temper," Sage observed as he stooped to gather up the items.

While he rolled up the door, Sage and I crept closer. Out of nowhere a thunderous bang filled the air. The sound ricocheted off the metal walls and echoed through the storage yard. Gunshots? An explosion? I couldn't tell.

The man tossed aside the food and drink he was carrying and dropped to the ground, covering his face with his arms.

CHAPTER 22

ROSEMARY

When I heard the man crunching over the gravel, I'd passed out the broken halves of the antacid tablets—four halves each to Mom, Dad, and Special Agent Morgan. I kept six halves for my bottle. We dropped them into the four empty water bottles we'd set aside and then I poured half a bottle of the hottest water we had into each bottle.

"Tighten the cap then shake," I whispered when I heard the key in the padlock.

I waited for the door to roll up, my fizzing water bottle in hand. But something must have gone awry outside because there was a lot of banging, swearing in a foreign language, and a resounding kick aimed at the door. So, we just kept shaking. In the end, it was that delay that served us so well.

By the time the metal door rose and the man stepped into view, the pressure in our bottles had reached maximum capacity.

I threw my bottle at his feet and, even though I'd obviously known the launch was coming, when the water bottle shot up from the floor and exploded loudly against the roof of the storage unit, I froze. It was a spectacular display, if I do say so myself.

The man yelped and rolled himself into a ball on the ground, protecting his eyes as if he expected flares or smoke bombs.

As soon as he was down, I shouted, "Now!"

I ran past him as Mom, Dad, and Special Agent Morgan tossed the three backup rockets we'd made on the ground near him. Then we sprinted away from the pod as all three water bottles rocked and, one after another, soared into the sky. At least one of them broke apart from the force of the reaction, and bits of plastic and hot, bubbling water rained down on our captor.

"Where's the pickup?" I called to my father, looking around wildly.

"I don't know where they put it, honey." He gave me a helpless look.

I turned back to see if the truck might be parked behind the storage unit. It wasn't, but my timing was perfect and I got to watch Special Agent Morgan stop beside our captor and put his foot down firmly on the man's back. "You have the right to remain silent," he began.

First, I gaped in amazement that Colin Morgan, who'd been captured by the baseball bat-wielding thug, after all, had screwed up his courage to apprehend the man. If I had to guess, the adrenaline pouring through his body in the wake of the explosions and our escape had spurred him to action.

Next, I wondered if an IRS computer guy could really officially Mirandize a suspect. But I quickly decided the legalities, such as they were, fell squarely under 'Not My Problem.'

Just then, Sage and Thyme emerged from behind a gleaming silver trailer. I blinked, shook my head, and stared at them in disbelief.

"What are you doing here?" I asked.

My parents turned and saw Thyme and Sage. Dad's mouth fell open.

"Girls!" Mom said, shocked. "You shouldn't be here."

"We're rescuing you," Sage informed me.

"Oh. Well, you're a little late. We just rescued ourselves."

She laughed. "What was that commotion, anyway?"

"Remember when I showed Skylar and Dylan how to make a rocket with water and baking soda?"

"Sure." She gave me a quizzical look. "You exploded water bottles?"

"More or less," I told her.

"Wait, where'd you get baking soda?" Thyme wanted to know.

"Dad's antacids."

"Chemistry saves the day, eh?" Thyme said with a grin. Then she dangled a set of keys hanging from a rental company keychain. "How about a ride back to the resort?"

Dad's eyes bulged out. "Yes, let's get out of here. Special Agent Morgan can handle that thug. We need to vamoose before Herk comes out to see what all the racket is. I'm surprised he's not out here already, to be honest."

"Oh, don't worry, Dad," Thyme said. "The guys are taking care of Herk."

I froze. "The guys? Our guys?"

"Yep. Dave, Roman, and Victor are in Herk's office, pretending to be interested in renting a storage spot. Let's get a safe distance away—there's a gas station across the road. Then we'll stop and call to let the guys know you're safe. They'll extricate themselves, and your new friend can arrest Herk and his henchman while we're all back at the resort, toasting marshmallows over the fire pit," Sage said with a smile.

I dug my bare toes into the ground. "I'm not leaving them here."

"Rosie, they're distracting Herk specifically so we can get you out of here," Thyme explained in a patient voice.

"I don't care. I'm not leaving without Dave," I insisted petulantly. Now that the immediate danger was over, I was trembling with emotion. And there was simply no way I was going anywhere without Dave.

After a moment, Sage nodded. "You've had a difficult day. We'll do this your way. Thyme, why don't you take Mom and Dad home. I'll wait here with Rosemary."

Mom and Dad exchanged glances over my

head. Then my mother said, "No. This has gone on long enough. Let's go talk to Herk."

It was clear she was talking specifically to our dad, but Sage, Thyme, and I tripped along behind them. I ended up in between my sisters. Wordlessly, we entwined our elbows, just as we had when they'd walked me down the aisle hours earlier during the wedding rehearsal.

"Thanks for coming for me," I said softly.

"As if we wouldn't," Sage answered with a smile.

"Yeah, how could we have a wedding without the bride? You don't think we made all those favor bags for our health, do you?" Thyme cracked.

I laughed, but it occurred to me that Thyme had inherited Dad's stupid jokes gene.

Behind us, Special Agent Morgan was hauling our now subdued captor, who was apparently named Yuri, toward the office as well. It was shaping up to be quite a party.

CHAPTER 23

SAGE

*W*e trooped into Herk's office, where he was apparently giving the guys the hard sell on an enclosed storage spot. Judging by the bored expression on Roman's face, the spiel had been going on for a while.

"Rosemary!" Dave shouted.

She flew across the room and buried her face in his chest. He circled his arms around her and pulled her tight.

"Yuri!" Herk roared.

Herk and Yuri's reunion was somewhat less tender than Rosemary and Dave's. The sulking hulk of a man glowered silently from his spot just inside the door while Herk pounded on his desk and demanded that Yuri do something about us.

While Herk sputtered, my parents worked the room, pumping first Roman's and then Victor's hand in an enthusiastic greeting. (Dave was still otherwise occupied reuniting with his betrothed.)

Thyme and Special Agent Morgan were having a loud, animated discussion about Herk's many financial crimes.

As a rule, I don't have a lot of sympathy for Herk but I could certainly relate to the sour expression on his face. All the shouting and frenzied activity in the tight, cramped space gave me an instant headache. So, like a modern-day Mary Poppins, I dug into my bottomless nanny bag of tricks to solve the problem.

I reached over and flipped the light switch on the wall. *Off. On. Off.*

Instant silence followed. I smiled to myself and turned the lights back on. That little move always worked like a charm. It was as foolproof as my second-favorite way to quell a din: whispering. Which is what I did next.

"People, let's calm down and talk one at a time," I suggested in a hushed tone so everyone had to strain to hear me. "I think we should start with introductions."

I cut my eyes to Special Agent Morgan.

"I'm Colin Morgan, SA-CIS with the IRS. Mr. Andrenko here has had his rights read to him and has wisely decided to zip his lips until the local police arrive."

"You called the cops?" I asked, worried.

"Not yet," he answered just loud enough for me to hear. "Although Yuri did return my cell phone. I figure I'll wait until you and your parents have left to bring in the boys in blue."

My eyes widened. "What are you saying?"

He blushed. "I've been fairly obsessed with nabbing your parents. But having spent some time trapped in a metal box with them and your sister, they suddenly seem real to me. And they risked everything to come to her wedding—a wedding they weren't even invited to. It doesn't seem right to haul them off before they get a chance to see her walk down the aisle."

"You mean, you'll let them come to the wedding?"

He nodded. "We talked through it while we were stuck in the pod. I'm going to stick pretty close to them, just so they don't get a sudden urge to travel. But my department doesn't even know

I'm here. I was doing this on my own time. Tomorrow, after you've all had a chance to celebrate, I'll take them in."

My face must have fallen a bit at the phrase 'take them in,' because he hurriedly added, "I don't think they'll do much, if any jail time. They're ready to face the music, accept responsibility, and make restitution."

"They are?" I asked, unable to hide my surprise. I mean, my parents are loveable, old hippies, but they've never been paragons of virtuous responsibility.

He nodded. "They are."

Herk was squinting at us. "So, if you're finished chatting up your lady friend, G-Man, I'm wondering what business you have with me? Do I need to call my tax attorney?"

Everything about Herk was oily. His voice, his hair, his very manner. I felt a small, involuntary shiver of disgust creep along my spine at his extreme unctuousness.

Special Agent Morgan stared at Herk for a long moment then said, "My colleagues on the Organized Crime Task Force will have all sorts of 'business' with you. But your primary concern should be the multiple kidnapping charges you'll be facing. So, to answer your question, you shouldn't bother calling your tax attorney, but you better hope you have a criminal defense attorney on speed dial."

Dad cleared his throat. Nobody paid any attention to him. So then he fake coughed. No reaction.

"Dad wants to say something," I announced.

Everyone crammed into the room turned to face my father as best they could.

"Thanks, honey." He smiled nervously. "First of all, thank you all for coming together to look for Rosemary. My daughters are lucky to have one another, and you men, to rely on, especially while their mother and I have been out of reach." He paused and squared his shoulders. "Mary Jane and I came here in an effort to rescue Rosemary because we know we're responsible for putting her in this situation—"

"Does that mean you have my ransom money after all?" Herk asked.

I'd always thought 'he made my skin crawl' was just an expression. But, nope. My skin actually felt as if it were crawling with creepy, crawly things when Herk spoke. He was so vile.

"No, Herk, there's no money for you," my mom said, jutting out her chin. "But we've made a decision. Instead of treating our financial situation like a shameful secret we have to hide, we're going to bring it all out into the open. All of it."

Dad picked up the thread. "That means your pressure tactics, your threats and blackmail, will all become public knowledge, Herk. So even if the people of Seashore didn't already know the kind of man you are, they definitely will going forward."

If I hadn't seen it with my own eyes, I never would have believed it, but Herk's face grew ruddy and flushed. He was embarrassed. The moment passed quickly and morphed into rage.

"I'll ruin you," he promised.

My dad smiled beatifically. "Goodbye, Herk."

"Can we leave?" Mom asked Special Agent Morgan.

He nodded. "Just remember our agreement. Go right back to the resort and stay there. I'll be along as soon as the police are done here. Rosemary, they're going to need to interview you, of course. Actually, they'll probably want to talk to all of you. But I can throw my federal law enforcement weight around to convince them to wait until after the reception tomorrow."

Rosemary grinned. "Thanks. And try to wrap it up quickly here, Special Agent Morgan. It's going to be all hands on deck in the kitchen tonight."

CHAPTER 24

THYME

For someone who didn't want help with her cake, Rosemary sure seemed to be enjoying having a team in her kitchen. Dad had uncorked a couple bottles of wine, and Mom had fired up her folk music playlist. Sage and Roman were slow dancing to some Carole King song and generally getting in the way. I thought someone should remind them that they were supposed to be juicing lemons, but I held my tongue.

Rosemary set Victor to work whipping an enormous bowl of lavender cream by hand while Dave and Special Agent Morgan each manned a vat of honeysuckle-infused simple syrup.

Mom and I were crystallizing flowers for the

cake topper under Rosemary's watchful eye. Dad had somehow managed to get out of doing any real work and was sitting on the counter with Parsley in his lap, a glass of red in his hand, and a bemused expression on his face, as if he wasn't quite sure how he'd ended up here. I knew the feeling.

Mom tilted her head toward Sage and Roman. "They seem happy."

"They are," I answered absently, trying to get a violet to dry straight and not all wrinkly for once. I snuck a look at Mom's growing heap of flowers. They were all perfect. Then I turned my attention to my own pitiful pile. I figured Rosemary could artfully hide mine under the good ones.

"And Roman's a good man?" she pressed.

It occurred to me that it was probably wildly disconcerting to come home and find your three daughters involved in serious relationships with three men you'd never even laid eyes on. I put down the flower and gave Mom my full attention.

"Roman *is* a good man. He was a history major in school, but he's a very talented golfer. It's in his genes, I guess. His dad's on the PGA Tour. Sage works for the dad's family as an attachment parenting consultant."

Mom frowned. Dad, who was eavesdropping from his corner, said, "A who what now?"

"A nanny. But she shares parenting ideas that aren't really mainstream. You know, co-sleeping, nonviolent communication, free-range learning. All the hippie stuff you guys did."

My mother and father exchanged proud smiles.

"Dave, your soon-to-be son-in-law, is also a good man. He's a Southern gentleman and a homicide detective. He's the gentlest guy you'd ever want to meet. And he's an animal lover."

"Cats?" Dad asked. Parsley purred and opened one eye, awaiting my answer.

"Um, dogs, actually. He and Rosemary have a dog named Mona Lisa, and they volunteer at some shelter near Los Angeles."

Dad nodded. Parsley hissed.

"And what about Victor?" Mom wanted to know.

"Victor's awesome. He's Brazilian. He came here to go to college. He put himself through school working as a driver, and then he went to J-school to—"

"J-school?"

"Journalism school. He's a financial reporter for *The New York Times.*"

"And how did you two meet, pumpkin?" Dad asked.

"I used to work with his sister. She went missing, and I helped him find her."

"Ha, and now he's helped you find your missing sister. How symmetrical," my mom observed.

I nodded. "Things have worked out pretty perfectly, really. Victor comes from a big, close-knit family. He's always been sort of sad that he wouldn't get the chance to meet you. But now he has."

My mother smiled. "And I'm glad to be able to meet him. He asked Dad to take a walk with him tomorrow. Very Old World."

I just nodded because I had literally zero idea what she was talking about.

Rosemary shooed Sage and Roman out of her way and opened the big wall oven, which had been preheating for some time. A blast of hot air filled the room. She and Dave carefully eased the five layers for her cake inside and gently closed the door.

Victor caught my eye and mimed rubbing his

bicep. I stifled a laugh. Whipping cream by hand was muscle-burning work.

"I think that's good, gang," Rosemary announced. "After the cakes have baked and cooled, I'll assemble and frost them. But the hard work's done. Thank you. All of you."

Just then Kay opened the door and peeked in. "Rosemary? Chelle's here. She wants to know if she can have your dress to clean and press it for tomorrow. She understands it might be ... dusty."

"Sure." Rosemary tossed her room key toward Kay, who snagged it out of the air one-handed. "And tell her thanks."

Kay nodded. Then she caught sight of Special Agent Morgan. "Mr. Morgan, I've booked you into the Petunia Cottage, right next door to Mr. and Mrs. Simon—er, Field. Is that okay?"

"That's perfect," he assured her.

Even the fact that my fugitive parents were under the watchful eye of a federal agent couldn't dampen my mood. The scene in the kitchen, as loopy and unexpected as it was, had a very familiar, comforting feeling; it felt like family.

CHAPTER 25

ROSEMARY

By rights, I should have been exhausted. I'd stayed up past one o'clock in the morning, cleaning up the kitchen and reminiscing with my parents and sisters about growing up at the resort.

Then, I'd leapt from bed at five-thirty on the dot this morning, just minutes before the Dowell's rooster ushered in the sunrise. By seven o'clock, I'd frosted, assembled, and decorated the cakes. By eight, I'd read over my vows for the thirty billionth time, showered, and washed and dried my hair.

Now, all that was left was the waiting.

"Maybe you should take a nap?" Sage suggested.

I gave her a look. "I'm too excited to sleep."

Thyme, who was arranging my blonde hair into a cascade of thick spirals that she piled into a high bun and secured with a glittering comb, met my eyes in the mirror. "You've got several hours to kill, Rosemary."

"I know. I thought the three of us could go to the fairy garden."

Sage threw a panicked look at my newly cleaned gown and the two spotless strapless dresses she and Thyme would be wearing. (One light purple, one light green).

"Don't worry," I assured her. "We can go before we change. Please? It'll be fun."

"I'm game," Thyme said with a little shrug of her shoulders.

"Why not," Sage agreed.

So the three of us slipped out through the French doors that had caused me so much grief just yesterday and wound our way along the path that followed a hill down behind the back of the house. The fairy garden wasn't the sort you sometimes see on manicured lawns, with whimsical, glittery stone houses and darling terra cotta decorations. Our fairy garden was an overgrown jumble of wild-flowers surrounding an old tree stump with a hole in it.

We'd discovered it when I was six or seven. We were absolutely convinced fairies used the tree stump as a portal to commute between our world and theirs. We used to pack up a lunch and spend hours sitting cross-legged in the patch of flowers just waiting for a fairy sighting and spinning stories about the fairies. Every once in a while, we'd find some berries or an acorn a bird had dropped and decide that the fairies had left them there as a message for us.

Standing there now, I felt like that little girl with perpetually scraped elbows and knees and two braids bumping against my shoulders and not like a fully grown woman who ran two businesses and was about to make a commitment to the man who shared her life.

I glanced over at my sisters. Thyme was humming under her breath. I recognized the tune; it was a song we'd made up for the fairies. Sage was crouched beside the tree stump, peering into the hole as if she'd resumed our decades-old vigil.

"I wanted to tell you both something about Mom and Dad," I said.

Thyme stopped humming, and Sage stood up slowly. They watched me, waiting for me to elaborate, so I did.

"Yesterday, while we were trapped in that storage unit, we had a lot of time to talk. And they told me they'd saved several thousand dollars. You know those two, they weren't exactly sure how much. But they said they wanted to give it to us so we could reinvest it in the resort."

Sage frowned. "It's a lot of money, for sure. I know because I saw it in the cottage when Roman and I were searching for clues about what happened to you. There was a giant stack of cash in Dad's underwear drawer."

Of course there was. That sounded just like our father.

"We shouldn't take it, though. They need to use that to pay off their other debts. I mean, right?" Thyme interjected.

"I think they will," Sage agreed. "I spoke briefly to Special Agent Morgan about the possibility of a settlement with the government. Besides, I think it gets messy if we take their money for the resort."

"Me, too. So I told them no. This place belongs to the three of us now. And it's finally becoming something other than a weight around our necks. But I was thinking we could offer them jobs helping us manage things. They could live here and work with Kay, so we wouldn't have to make so many trips back to check on things. How do you two feel about that?"

Thyme answered first. "I think it's a great idea, so long as they aren't handling the finances in any way."

"I think they've finally realized that's not their strong suit, but I agree. Kay would remain in charge of the accounts, but they could help with reservations, maintenance, guests' requests—that sort of thing," I said.

Sage looked first at me and then at Thyme. "Does this mean you two are ready to forgive them? Can we be a family again?" Her eyes were shining.

"I hope so," I said. "It's what I want."

"So do I," Thyme chimed in. "You were right, Sage. We do need to forgive them and move forward."

She grinned at us. "It took you two long enough to come around." Then she had a thought. "Do you want them to walk you down the aisle instead of us?"

I shook my head, making the curls bounce wildly. "No. You two are walking with me; you've earned that. I have an idea, though."

At precisely four o'clock, I stood under the elm tree in my magically fresh, clean, and pressed wedding gown, clutching a bouquet of flowers that had just been picked from the garden and tied off with a silk ribbon. My left arm was linked through Sage's and my right was linked through Thyme's, just as we'd rehearsed. But now, Sage's left arm was linked through our mother's arm, and Thyme's right was linked through our father's.

We'd rearranged the chairs to make a *much* wider aisle and had convinced Marie to switch out the processional music. As she pluck the first cords of "Bridge Over Troubled Water" on her harp, the five us stepped in unison onto the petal-strewn path that would lead me to my future with Dave.

Chelle and Kay were both already crying when our unwieldy human chain passed their seats. Special Agent Morgan gave us a thumbs up from his spot between Roman and Victor. And my Aunt Ruby was blowing her nose into Uncle Joe's hand-kerchief, sounding like a loud, angry goose.

We reached the gazebo and Thyme and Sage released my arms and each fell back a step. Mom and Dad came around and kissed me on the cheek before taking their seats.

Dave stood alone under the canopy of blooms and fairy lights. His familiar smile and the expectant gleam in his eyes almost undid me right there, and I was afraid I'd end up doing a honking duet with Aunt Ruby. Then he winked at me, and my heart melted.

I reached for his hand and squeezed it tightly while Reverend Mark greeted our friends and families. The ceremony was a blur. I tried to concentrate on what Mark was saying, and the meanings of the readings my sisters had chosen to mark the occasion, but it was impossible to focus.

I'm marrying Dave. I'm marrying Dave.

The sentence spooled around and around in my mind. My heart seemed to beat in time with its cadence.

I'm marrying Dave. I'm marrying Dave.

And then, through the haze of my emotion, I heard Mark saying it was time to recite our vows and exchange our rings.

A few minutes later, Dave was covering my mouth for a quick kiss full of promise and love. And just like that, I was his wife. He was my husband. We were married. We were family.

CHAPTER 26

SAGE

I flitted around the reception tent, making sure all the details were perfect. And they were.

People were eating, drinking, and dancing under the twinkling lights. A cluster of Dave's cousins' children gathered around the S'mores bar, squealing with sugar-induced glee. Reverend Mark, who had a fierce sweet tooth, had graciously volunteered to supervise the toasting of the marshmallows over a table of Bunsen burners Rosemary had borrowed from the high school's science department.

The mason jars filled with wildflowers picked up the light from the globes strung above the tables. The mismatched, vintage china in several faded patterns looked fabulous against the simple white tablecloths. I was pretty darn impressed. Thyme had done a great job.

Speaking of Thyme, where was she? I scanned the tent and spotted her. She and Victor were twirling around the dance floor like their names were Fred and Ginger. Meanwhile, Rosemary and Dave were weaving their way through the tables, hand in hand, stopping to chat with everyone and to show off their wedding rings.

The only thing missing was my date.

Roman seemed to have disappeared. I searched the tent carefully but saw no sign of him. After a moment, I realized my parents and Special Agent Morgan were also nowhere to be seen.

I suppressed a groan. It hadn't even been twenty-four hours since Rosemary had vanished. Surely the family wasn't due for another abduction already?

I popped a small round of toasted bread smeared with roasted fig jam into my mouth to distract myself from *that* line of thought and plucked a flute of champagne from a silver tray.

I was sipping it and chatting with Chelle, when I spotted Roman headed toward the tent. He was coming up the walking path from the meditation garden. And he wasn't alone. My parents were with him, and Special Agent Morgan trailed behind them.

I excused myself from the conversation with Chelle and raced over to him.

"Is everything okay?" I asked anxiously as soon as I reached him. The last thing Rosemary and Dave needed at their reception was more parental drama.

He gave me a puzzled look. "Everything's fine," he squeaked in a strangely high, tight voice. He coughed and cleared his throat.

My mother tittered. Dad pulled her away from us and hurried over to join Aunt Ruby and Uncle Joe at their table.

I watched them walk away then turned back to Roman. "What were you and my parents doing?"

"Just chatting. Oh, look, scallops!"

He darted toward the caterer who was circulating with the tray of scallops as though she were handing out PGA tour cards on a first come, first served basis.

I trotted after him. "Are you sure nothing's wrong?" I demanded.

He swallowed his scallop and caught me in his arms. "I'm positive," he breathed near my ear.

His mouth tickled my ear and I shivered. Roman pressed closer.

"In fact," he continued, "everything is perfect." He swooped down and kissed the hollow of my throat. "You're perfect. Now, may I have this dance?"

I had a strong suspicion I was being distracted, but I was happy to be distracted. So I let him lead me out onto the dance floor. As we moved in time to the music, his weird behavior faded from my mind. I rested my head on his shoulder and allowed myself to relax into his arms.

CHAPTER 27

THYME

*V*ictor rubbed my sore feet. I leaned back against the headboard of the bed and gave a contented sigh as his strong fingers worked my tired muscles.

"Thank you," I breathed. "That was the most fun I've ever had at a wedding, but I think I did too much dancing."

Victor popped up from the floor in mock outrage. "Too much dancing? In Brazil, we don't even have a phrase for too much dancing!"

I giggled. "Wouldn't that be ... *muita dança?*"

I'd been trying to learn Portuguese so I could talk to his extended family when we visited them in the fall. Let's just say my rusty Spanish wasn't much help in my endeavor.

He beamed at me like a proud teacher. "Lots of dancing is probably the closer translation, but I give you an A for effort." He leaned in and kissed me.

My foreign language lessons came with lots of perks. Mainly kisses. And the occasional foot massage. Accordingly, I was a highly motivated student.

"Oh, did you talk to my parents?" I asked.

Once Victor had learned Mr. and Mrs. Simon, the bird lovers, were really my mom and dad, he'd insisted he had to talk to them about our upcoming trip to Brazil. I told him it was unnecessary, but he'd refused to be swayed. I thought it was adorably archaic of him to make sure my parents approved of our trip. I just needed to make sure he didn't make a habit of asking for their approval. I was, after all, an adult.

"I did. I had to get in line, but I did get their blessing for the trip."

"What do you mean, you had to get in line?" I asked.

"Roman beat me to it. He got the first audience with them tonight," he explained.

Audience? Forget Portuguese, I was starting to wonder if I understood English.

"My dad's not the Pope—and my mom's not the Queen. Why would Roman need an audience with them?"

"What?" Victor said.

"What do you mean, what?"

"I didn't hear what you said."

Even though I was pretty sure he knew exactly what I'd just said, I started to repeat myself. But he eased me back onto the bed and stopped my mouth with a kiss. And then another. And yet another.

"What did Roman need to talk to my parents about?" I asked, trying again.

But by now his lips had moved to my neck, and I was rapidly losing interest in the conversation. I cradled his head in my hands, weaving my fingers through his thick, dark hair, and promptly forgot all about audiences—papal, royal, and especially parental.

CHAPTER 28

ROSEMARY — MONDAY

The resort was quiet. After three days of celebration and joyful chaos, the silence and stillness were both welcome and disconcerting. Sage and Roman and Thyme and Victor had stuck around to say goodbye to our parents after all the guests had cleared out. But even they had left last night. They all had to get back to work.

After breakfast, Special Agent Morgan had made himself scarce so Dave and I could say goodbye to my parents in private. It had been a more hopeful, less tearful parting than I'd expected. Mom and Dad were eager to resolve their legal troubles, and they trusted Colin to treat them fairly.

Because of the giant pile of state and federal criminal charges that Herk the Jerk was facing, my parents were going to be important witnesses for the prosecution in multiple cases. Special Agent Morgan assured us their cooperation wouldn't go unrewarded.

So, when the government-issued car pulled out from the long circular driveway, my heart was surprisingly light. Dave wrapped his arm around my waist. The morning sun warmed my bare shoulders. A rose-breasted grosbeak perched in the tree near the porch sang, and the wind carried its song, rich and sweet and melodious, on the air.

We watched the car disappear from view. After a moment, Dave turned to me and grinned.

"So, I suppose the honeymoon starts now, Mrs. Drummond. What would my wife like to do today?"

I rested my head on his shoulder. "I'd love to go down to the beach and watch the tide roll in with my husband."

"That can be arranged," he said, catching my earlobe playfully between his teeth. "Any other requests?"

I pressed my palms against his chest and stretched up to kiss him then teasingly said, "Oh, I have lots of requests, Mr. Drummond. But there's no hurry. We have the place to ourselves until Wednesday."

A slow smile spread across his face and he pulled me tight. "Two whole days with no crimes to solve, no events to cater, and no dog to walk. I don't know how we'll pass the time."

I put on a serious face and said, "My husband's inordinately clever and creative. I'm sure he'll think of something."

Then I dissolved into giggles and took off running toward the beach. Dave caught up with me halfway there and swooped me into his arms to carry me the rest of the way.

Much, much later, when the afternoon sun was high in the sky, we returned to our room to remove sand from body parts that had no business being sandy. We were soaking in the oversized clawfoot tub and listening to the waves crash down on the shore, when my cell phone rang.

I reached for it on the vanity.

"Ignore it," he urged, as he gently pulled me back into the water.

I hesitated for a half-second before sinking back into the foamy bubbles with a satisfied smile. I rested my head on his broad chest and leaned against him.

We stayed in the tub until we realized we hadn't eaten since breakfast. By the time we got out, the water had turned cold and the bubbles were just a sudsy memory. I could almost hear the bed calling my name.

After I wrapped myself in a thick robe, I remembered my missed call. I listened to my voice-mail message once, then a second time. Then I sprawled on the bed next to Dave, who looked as though he was also contemplating taking an early evening nap.

"Who called?" he asked.

"A potential client. She's looking for someone to cater a destination wedding."

"I thought you were never catering another wedding again," he teased. "Isn't that what you said after the Steinbrenner-Moskowitz shindig?"

"I did say that," I agreed. "But this bride has very specifically requested my honeysuckle lemon cake with lavender cream for her wedding reception."

He turned on to his side and gave me a surprised look. "Would you really make *our* cake for someone else? Can't you suggest different flavors?"

I felt my mouth curve into a smile.

"I could. But it sounded as if Sage and Roman already have their minds made up."

THANK YOU!

Thanks for reading *Lost and Gowned!* Ready for more of the Field sisters? The sisters are back in *Wedding Bells and Hoodoo Spells*, the next book in this series.

Keep reading. You can always find an up-to-date list of the titles in this series, as well as the books in my other series, on my website, www.melissafmiller.com.

Sign up. While you're at my website, sign up for my email newsletter to be the first to know when I have a new release. In addition to new release alerts, subscribers receive notices of sales and other book news, goodies, and exclusive subscriber bonuses.

Review it. I'd love it if you'd head back to where you bought this book and consider posting a short review to help other readers decide whether they might enjoy it.

ALSO BY MELISSA F. MILLER

Want to know when I release a new book?

Go to www.melissafmiller.com to sign up for my email
newsletter.

The Sasha McCandless Legal Thriller Series

Irreparable Harm

Inadvertent Disclosure

Irretrievably Broken

Indispensable Party

Lovers and Madmen (Novella)

Improper Influence

A Marriage of True Minds (Novella)

Irrevocable Trust

Irrefutable Evidence

A Mingled Yarn (Novella)

Informed Consent

International Incident

Imminent Peril

The Humble Salve (Novella)

The Aroostine Higgins Novels

Critical Vulnerability

Chilling Effect

Calculated Risk

Called Home

The Bodhi King Novels

Dark Path

Lonely Path

Hidden Path

The We Sisters Three Romantic Comedic Mysteries

Rosemary's Gravy

Sage of Innocence

Thyme to Live

Lost and Gowned

ACKNOWLEDGMENTS

As always, I'm grateful to my editing team for putting the polish on my work. I'm also wildly lucky to have a husband and children who support my writing, especially around deadline time!

ABOUT THE AUTHOR

USA Today bestselling author Melissa F. Miller was born in Pittsburgh, Pennsylvania. Although life and love led her to Philadelphia, Baltimore, Washington, D.C., and, ultimately, South Central Pennsylvania, she secretly still considers Pittsburgh home.

In college, she majored in English literature with concentrations in creative writing poetry and medieval literature and was STUNNED, upon graduation, to learn that there's not exactly a job market for such a degree. After working as an editor for several years, she returned to school to earn a law degree. She was that annoying girl who loved class and always raised her hand. She practiced law for fifteen years, including a stint as a clerk for a federal judge, nearly a decade as an attorney at major international law firms, and several years running a two-person law firm with her lawyer husband.

Now, powered by coffee, she writes legal thrillers and homeschools her three children. When she's not writing, and sometimes when she is, Melissa travels around the country in an RV with her husband, her kids, and her cat.

Connect with me:
www.melissafmiller.com

www.ingramcontent.com/pod-product-compliance
Lightning Source LLC
Chambersburg PA
CBHW051244250626
47155CB00009B/3153